"Are you ready to have a baby?" Matt asked

"What? I don't think being a single parent is the best idea in the world."

"I could be the father of your children," he said blandly. "Might be your best chance."

Peta's mouth fell into a very sensual pout as she dragged in a deep breath. Matt was tempted to step forward and kiss her, get her mind moving on a positive path. He thought better of it.

"I've had a hard time finding a woman who wants to be a wife and mother."

"You just want to have sex with me."

"Can't have kids without doing it," he said cheerfully. "All I ask is that you give it some thought."

Peta turned and marched off.

"See you at dinner," Matt called after her. She didn't reply, didn't glance back. He didn't expect her to. She was in shock. But, given time, the seeds he'd planted in her mind would start to grow. After all, he and she wanted the same thing.

Welcome to MAN TALK! A wonderful miniseries featuring some of your favorite Presents™ authors— Charlotte Lamb, Sandra Field, Alison Kelly and Emma Darcy—all written from the hero's point of view.

Find out what men really think about sex, love and relationships. And when these guys talk, you'll want to listen.... This month it's Emma Darcy's turn to invite you to share in a little MAN TALK!

*There are two sides to every relationship...
and now it's his turn!*

Emma Darcy

Fatherhood Fever!

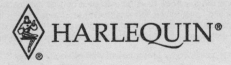

HARLEQUIN®

TORONTO • NEW YORK • LONDON
AMSTERDAM • PARIS • SYDNEY • HAMBURG
STOCKHOLM • ATHENS • TOKYO • MILAN • MADRID
PRAGUE • WARSAW • BUDAPEST • AUCKLAND

ISBN 0-373-11984-4

FATHERHOOD FEVER!

First North American Publication 1998.

CHAPTER ONE

IF ONLY you'd give me a grandchild I'd have something to live for.

His mother's words tapped a deep well of frustration. Matt Davis was so irritated by them, he headed for the open air and lit a cigarette, defiantly dragging in a soothing shot of nicotine and belligerently crushing the guilt of breaking his resolution to give up the hazardous habit of smoking. Right at this moment, a death wish didn't seem so bad.

He strolled towards the garden, brooding over his failure to prompt his mother into doing something positive for herself. Ever since his father's death, she'd been wallowing in a pit of depression, letting herself go, unable to summon the energy or interest to pursue an active life. Bringing her to this health farm had seemed like a good idea but it wasn't working the miracle he'd hoped for. She was enjoying the pampering treatments he'd organised—trying out a Reiki massage right now—but it wasn't raising any significant will to forge a new path for herself.

It was absurd to hang the rest of her life on his having children. There were plenty of other ways to fill the void of widowhood. She was only fifty-five, for God's sake! And she could be so attractive when she was firing on all cylinders. His father wouldn't have wanted her to mourn him forever. If she'd get out more, *do* things. A *grandchild*, of course, didn't require her to do anything. It was more like a gift from heaven falling into her lap.

Except it wasn't quite so easy to provide!

Matt paused at the stone steps into the garden and took another angry drag on the smouldering cigarette. He watched the smoke drift into the cool, crisp air and swirl away on the wind. Gone, he thought, like the time of his mother's generation when women were content to be wives and mothers. Those he'd been closely involved with regarded having children as an unwelcome curtailment of their freedom, not to be entered into until they were *ready*.

His mouth twisted in savage irony. *He* was ready. At thirty-three, he was more than ready to become a father. He'd done the freewheeling bachelor bit and was finding the life increasingly empty. His ambition on the work-front was more than satisfied. The merchandising business he'd started and developed was now a solid money-spinner, ensuring financial security for the foreseeable future. He wasn't exactly lonely, but the appeal of having his own family to share everything with was strong.

He was sure he'd be a good dad, like his own father. The thought brought a flood of memories and a sudden bolt of grief. His mother wasn't the only one who missed the old man. Matt heaved a sigh to relieve the ache of loss and sternly told himself life moved on. It had to. There was no going back to those happy times with his father.

Unfortunately, his mother's simplistic belief that he could get himself married and start a family any time he liked was pure fantasy land in this day and age. Finding a woman willing to cooperate in such an old-fashioned life plan was akin to finding a needle in a haystack.

Everything else—careers, travel, living life to the full—came ahead of having a baby. Motherhood was too big a commitment of time and self to take on until a woman was *ready*. Both Janelle and Skye had told him so. To achieve the desirable end of fatherhood, it seemed he'd either have to find a woman in her early twenties who didn't know any better, or one in her late thirties whose biological clock was ticking. Neither idea was overly appealing.

He wanted...

The roar of a motorbike accelerating up the driveway blasted his train of thought. His head swivelled to the loud beast breaking the peace and quiet of the health farm. It was a shiny red, middleweight sportster. Matt automatically concentrated on identifying its make as it zoomed into the turning circle for arrivals—a Ducati 600 SS—very stylish Italian job.

It halted within a few metres of where he stood, still paused at the entrance to the garden. Only when the rider started to dismount did he realise it was a woman. His mind instantly clicked into appreciation mode. The black leathers moulded a fantastic female body, perfectly proportioned, deliciously curved and dynamically packed. A kick of excitement stirred hormones he'd thought had become jaded. This was one very sexy woman.

He watched with lively anticipation as she removed her helmet, then couldn't stop himself from staring outright at the stunning revelation of her face and hair. His riveted gaze did manage to register the pretty, rather gamine appeal of a delicately pointed chin and widely spaced cornflower blue eyes, separated by a finely flared nose and a lush mouth, but the hair totally transfixed him. Like a beacon it was, in blazing technicolour.

He'd never seen such vivid hair in his life. The gleaming copper cap was interrupted by two swathes of iridescent orange and gold, falling in precise bands around her head from a side parting. They glowed like two halos framing her face, set off by the copper bangs following the curve of her cheeks and the copper crown behind them.

The effect stimulated all sorts of wild ideas. This woman was not just sexy. She was dynamite—flaunting her daring, dabbling with danger, defying conventional standards, dumping any care of how others saw her, determined on dancing to her own tune, wherever it led her. She threw out a challenge that stirred more than Matt's hormones. It fired his blood and sizzled every sensible thought out of his brain.

He wanted…

"Okay to leave the bike here while I book in at reception?"

Her voice cut into the gathering maelstrom of desire, jolting him back to the real world. The bright blue eyes were regarding him derisively and Matt had the uncomfortable impression she knew precisely the nature of her impact on him and was darkly amused by it. Unaccustomed to being caught staring at anyone, he blathered his reply.

"Sure. It's safely out of the way of other incoming vehicles."

His voice sounded as though it was scraped out of a gravel pit. Very uncool.

Her mouth curled into a mocking smile. "Cheating, I see."

"What?" His mind had lost a gear somewhere.

"No smoking at this health farm," she tossed at him before turning to unstrap a bag from the bike.

He looked down at the offending cigarette, still alight between his fingers. He barely stopped the impulse to throw it away. Littering the ground with a burning butt would really be reprehensible. "I'm not hurting anyone, smoking outside," he excused.

"Guys always justify their cheating."

"And women don't?" he retorted, niggled by her cynical comment.

"I can't see any women out here polluting the pure crystalline air we're paying to breathe." She hefted the released bag onto her back and swung to eye him up and down consideringly. "But maybe you're staff, not paying at all. Aerobics instructor? Masseur?"

"Guest," he answered shortly, finding himself standing straighter under the boldly open appraisal of his length and breadth and the amount of muscle outlined by his tracksuit.

"For a macho man like you," she drawled, "this health farm must be a happy hunting ground. A bunch of women on the loose, needing to be fixed up."

Matt could not find his tongue. She stood like a provocative witch, her head tilted to one side, hair flaming around it, one hand holding the strap of her bag over her shoulder, the other planted on a seductively jutting hip, legs apart in a challenging stance, her black-leathered body taunting him with its sexy self-confidence.

"I bet you're just awesome when you strip," she went on, her eyes sparking with cold blue lights. "What any woman would call a gorgeous hunk. Do you work out with weights in the gym?"

It was a payback for the way he'd stared at her, pure and simple. When her gaze dropped pointedly to his crotch, Matt found his tongue very promptly. "I'm here with my mother."

It was a dumb thing to say, but at least it broke the focus of her attention on a highly volatile physical area. She looked up in startled bemusement. "A Mummy's boy?" Laughter bubbled out of her throat.

It fizzed through Matt's brain, exploding whatever common sense he had. "As maddening as my mother might be, I happen to care about her," he bit out, his jaw clenching over how foolish she made him feel.

"Well, good for you."

The sudden burst of warmth from her confused him further.

Sheer impishness shone from her broad grin and

she had the temerity to wink confidentially at him. "I hope you've got the stamina to keep on caring."

Then she was off, striding past him up the path to reception. Like an irresistible magnet she pulled his gaze after her. The brilliant copper cap bounced. Her jaunty walk kept changing the gleam on her leather-clad bottom, highlighting its cute cheekiness. Her legs seemed to spring with exciting vitality.

He yelped and dropped the cigarette. Damned thing had burnt his fingers. He bent to scoop up the smouldering butt and when he straightened, the glass doors to reception had swallowed up the tantalising torment that had invaded his space, turning him every which way.

He wondered what she'd be like in bed. He figured the sheets would be smoking with the heat she'd generate. He sure as hell wouldn't be thinking of having a cigarette. Or needing one.

With a self-derisive little laugh, he strolled on into the garden and buried the evidence of his *cheating,* vowing once again to stop the habit. He dragged in several deep breaths of the pure, crystalline air of the southern tablelands. The health farm was only two hours from Sydney, but it could have been a world away. He *should* be appreciating the total lack of pollution here.

A macho man like you... Was she impressed? Attracted to him? He hadn't been looking for a fling with any of the women guests, hadn't felt drawn to any of them, either, but this recent arrival certainly had him ticking over. He wondered how long she'd be staying and if he could keep his mother's eagle eye from noticing a change in his chemistry.

He glanced at the flamboyant, red Ducati. That was her baby. No way was the hell's angel who rode it *ready* for motherhood. He should give her a miss. She was bound to be trouble. If he got involved with her, his mother would look dolefully at him and complain, "You're just not trying, Matt."

If he wanted fatherhood, and he did—he really did—picking up with the wrong woman was stupidly self-defeating. On the other hand, a spin around the block on a Ducati wouldn't be wasting a lot of time. It might be time well spent. Excitingly spent.

A man only lived once.

There was no age limit on fatherhood.

It wasn't good for his mother to think a grandchild would answer everything.

Besides, he was not — definitely not — *a Mummy's boy!*

CHAPTER TWO

LENTILBURGERS!

Not to mention more rabbit food!

Matt's stomach growled a protest as he surveyed the lunch menu. What he'd give for a big juicy steak and a plate of French fries! His mouth salivated at the thought.

"Hungry, dear?" his mother said brightly. The Reiki massage had somehow perked up her energy level.

He forced a smile. "Starving." He piled four slices of freshly baked wholemeal bread onto his plate. At least that was filling.

"They do make such tasty salads here," his mother rattled on, helping herself to an avocado mix and lots of other greens as she moved along the buffet table.

It was good for her, Matt told himself. She'd piled on weight from comfort eating and needed to get herself back on a decent diet. If she left here with more of an interest in healthy food, at least he had achieved something. But it was no consolation to his stomach. He forked some tomato and onion onto his plate, added as many slices of boiled egg as he thought he could get away with, found some beetroot, and followed his mother to the table they'd been occupying, her at the foot of it, him next to her.

"Oh! Just look at that girl!"

The words were hissed at him as he sat down.

He looked, knowing from the shock in his mother's voice whom he'd see. He didn't expect to be drawn into staring at her again. But his eyes seemed to get glued on her and couldn't be wrenched away.

The black leather jacket had been removed. She wore a red sweater that clung like a second skin, showing off the superb slopes of two glorious breasts. Matt had never thought himself a breast man. Legs had always taken his fancy. He suddenly found himself converted. There was definitely a compelling attraction about perfectly rounded and fulsomely weighted breasts.

"I didn't think you could wear red with red," his mother murmured, her initial shock having turned to awed fascination.

"Mmmh…" he replied, leaving his response options open.

The vision of feminine plentitude moved past them to the buffet table, not so much as flicking a glance in his direction. Which was just as well, since being caught gawking at her again would have been galling. The cornflower blue eyes were quite capable of slicing him in two and shrivelling all activity below the belt. Though, come to think of it, his testosterone levels could probably do with a bit of shrivelling at the moment. Not since he was a teenager had he felt such a strong wave of lust.

"Well, *she's* new," his mother declared with relish,

her eyes atwinkle with more lively interest than she'd shown in anything for quite some time.

"Mmmh…" Matt repeated, busily buttering his bread. The communal table was filling up with the regulars. It usually held ten, though a couple of guests had departed this morning. He didn't want to be put on the spot with an open discussion of the new arrival. After all, he was the only male here and the focus of considerable speculation. He didn't really care to reveal how taken by her he was. Not when it was still uncertain how she felt about him. Now if she attended the archery session this afternoon…

"Don't you think she's striking?" his mother pressed.

"Quite," he agreed, stealthily withdrawing his personal salt cellar—a recent and desperate purchase from the grocery store in the nearby village—from his trouser pocket. Salt was not supplied at the health farm. He would suffer a lot for his mother, but doing without salt was taking sacrifice too far. He surreptitiously sprinkled it on his food while everyone else was still settling down to their meal.

"There's a spare chair here, dear," his mother called.

Matt couldn't believe his ears. His ultra-respectable, conservative mother inviting the sexy as sin, red on red to sit next to her? Opposite him? In the hot seat left by Vida, the vamp, who had gone through five husbands and had flirted with the idea of taking Matt as her toy-boy, much to his mother's amusement and his embarrassment?

He held his breath. She was coming, a whimsical little smile showing her surprise at the encouraging welcome extended by his mother. She cocked an eyebrow at Matt and he knew curiosity had drawn her. Mummy doing the honours for Mummy's boy?

"Thank you," she said, placing her plate on the table. "I was wondering where I should sit."

"There's no special place for anyone," his mother informed. "I'm Cynthia Davis. This is my son, Matt. And you are?"

"Peta. Peta Kelly."

Matt stood up to offer his hand in courtesy, only to realise he was still holding the salt cellar. She looked at it, looked at him, and rolled her eyes mockingly.

"Still at it, I see."

"At what?" his mother asked.

"Cheating. Your son was outside smoking when I arrived. Now he's sneaked in salt."

"Salt? Salt? Did someone say salt?" A plaintive voice cried from the other end of the table. "I'd give my eyeteeth for some salt."

Matt sighed and offered it up.

"Definitely a corrupting influence," Peta declared.

"And you are a spoilsport," he retorted in some exasperation. "A pity the jug on the table isn't full of prune juice. I could have offered you some."

She laughed and sat down. "Put out, are we?" she tossed at him teasingly.

"Matt, you promised to give up smoking…"

"Mum, if you nag me about one more thing today…"

"Well, if you want to have a baby…"

"*You* want to have a baby?" The cornflower blue eyes stared incredulously at him.

"Matt would make a wonderful father," his mother enthused.

"Pass the salt back, please," he thundered down the table.

"Salt? Who's got salt?" someone appealed from across the dining room.

"Got everyone cheating now," Peta muttered darkly.

Matt didn't care. At least he'd diverted the talk about babies. He gave his mother a baleful look. It was perfectly obvious babies were the last thing on Peta Kelly's mind. His freewheeling bachelor image would be far more likely to appeal to the rider of the red Ducati. If he was to get to first base with her, he had to shut his mother up on the subject of grandchildren. The problem was, she was so obsessive about it.

"Please forgive me," his mother gushed to the object of his desire. "I can't stop looking at your hair. I've never seen anything so daring."

Peta grinned at her. "Well, nobody can take me for a blond bimbo anymore."

More like a blond bombshell, Matt thought.

His mother was astonished. "You're really a blonde? I thought the copper red part was natural."

"Nope. Straight out of a bottle. It's called flaming chestnut."

"What are the other shades called?"

"The first band is crushed orange and behind it is papaya."

Very exotic, Matt thought. He reached for the jug of juice on the table and poured her a glass. "You'll like this. Tropical fruit."

She laughed. No mocking lights in her eyes this time. Pure amusement dancing at him. Matt's heart did cartwheels. There was definitely a connection here. He could feel it. He smiled at his mother.

"Why don't you do something exciting with your hair, Mum? Peach with cream highlights would look good. Much more fun than grey."

"Oh, Matt! I'm at the stage in life where there's nothing left to do but grow old gracefully."

"Nonsense! Who says the mature woman has to be dull? You admire Peta's daring. Put some colour into your hair. Splash out on some bright clothes to go with it. Start a new life."

"It can make you feel better," Peta said in support.

Matt grinned at her, delighted with her help in encouraging his mother to do something for herself. Peta looked quizzically at him, probably assessing his motives for using her as a glowing example to be emulated.

"Well, I'll think about it," his mother said dubiously.

It wasn't the usual flat negative. No negative vibrations coming from Peta, either. Matt sensed a burgeoning of interest. He munched into the sandwich he'd made with more appetite than he'd experienced for days.

"You must have a colourful job," his mother remarked to Peta, still in the grip of fascinated curiosity.

She shrugged, doing instant damage to Matt's resolution not to focus on her breasts. "Not really. I'm an airline stewardess with Qantas."

Fortunately his mother held Peta's attention. "On international flights?" she asked.

"Yes. Mostly to London or Rome."

Ah, the Italian influence, Matt thought.

"That must be a very responsible job, taking care of a planeload of people on such long trips," his mother said appreciatively.

Matt frowned. It was a fair comment. Somehow that kind of responsibility did not gell with the powerful sportster, black leathers and exotic hair. On the other hand, there was a lot of *action* in London and Rome. They could be very wild cities for those on the prowl for excitement.

"Yes. And it plays havoc with one's sleep patterns," she said. "Which is why I'm here. Maybe this place will help to regulate them."

Matt could think of other, more satisfying ways of regulating them than programmed exercises and lettuce leaves. He carefully kept his gaze lowered as his imagination took fire and hungered through several erotic fantasies.

"Try some massages, dear," his mother advised.

Yeah…slow and sensual would be great, Matt thought.

"I've just had the Reiki massage," his mother went on. "It does the most amazing transference of energy. The heat it generates in some places…"

Couldn't possibly be as good as sex.

"…I've had quite a lot of backache recently…"

Matt was jolted out of his private reverie. He frowned at his mother. "You didn't tell me that."

"Oh, you fuss so, Matt."

"You mean you don't want to hear that backache is often related to weight. And, of course, sitting around doing nothing instead of getting some proper exercise can exacerbate the problem."

"And you have the gall to call me a nag," she flared at him. "I'll have you know I didn't exercise when your father was alive, either."

"You didn't have to. You had a good sex-life."

"Oh!" That flustered her.

"Maybe Vida's right," Matt went on, enjoying his advantage. "Maybe I shouldn't have brought you to a health farm to encourage good habits. I should have got you a toy-boy instead."

"Matt! How could you? Your father…"

"My father would turn in his grave if he knew you'd given up on life, Mum. He loved a very vital woman who enjoyed herself in hundreds of ways. You might not miss that person but I do."

"Well, I certainly don't need a toy-boy." She was affronted.

Matt shrugged. "Just a thought."

"You think sex is the be-all and end-all, do you?" Peta drawled.

The cornflower blue eyes were very cutting, very cold, very cynical. Matt's spine crawled. This was a loaded question if ever he'd heard one, and coming from this red hot tomato, it had caught him right off-guard.

"No, I don't," he said. "But physically it can be a great workout." Extremely good for deep, restful sleep, he almost added.

The finely arched eyebrow lifted. "No need for weights at the gym to maintain that impressive physique?"

"Matt plays a lot of sport," his mother interposed.

"I bet he does. Sport would definitely be his thing." She smiled sweetly at him. "Do you cheat at that, too?"

There was arsenic in that smile.

His mother laughed. "Good heavens, no! Why would he? Matt's got so much natural talent, he's always been a winner," she declared proudly.

"Of course," Peta said dryly, and resumed her meal, closing off any further interest in the conversation.

The connection was broken. It was as decisive as a switch being thrown. Matt mused over it with mounting frustration. How could a woman who flaunted her assets be anti-sex? It made no sense to him yet that was the subject that had turned her off.

On the other hand, the continual dig about cheating might be significant. Maybe her last guy had cheated

on her. Some men were stupid. They'd stray anywhere with anyone available. Not him, though. Matt
worked on the principle…when you're onto a good
thing, stick to it.

He'd probably still be with Skye if she hadn't taken
that two-year contract overseas. He'd had quite a
long-term relationship with Janelle, too, until her career in law became more important than anything else.
Basically he was a one-woman man. He'd be very
happy to have Peta Kelly for as long as she wanted
him and he couldn't imagine even glancing at another
woman with her at his side.

Well, he'd straighten her out about him soon
enough. Maybe at the archery session. Shoot a few
arrows into the air…

"Do you play any sport, Peta?" his mother inquired, instantly pricking Matt's antenna for trouble.
Surely she wouldn't try her matchmaking tricks with
Peta Kelly. Couldn't she see this was not wife and
mother material?

The blue eyes flicked derisively at Matt before a
smile was turned on his mother. "I enjoy a game of
tennis."

Ah…mixed doubles, Matt thought with satisfaction.

"There's a round robin tennis session scheduled for
this afternoon. After archery," his mother informed.

"So I noticed."

"Matt's very good at tennis."

Another derisive look. "Maybe we'll get to drive
a few balls at each other."

"Mmmh..." said Matt, wondering why she was out for his blood. Not that it mattered. As far as he was concerned it was a definite date with her. One way or another, he was going to turn it to his advantage.

He smiled.

She smiled back.

The challenge was on.

And if his mother thought it might get her a grandchild, she was out of her tree!

CHAPTER THREE

"DOESN'T look like anyone else is coming," Matt cheerfully remarked.

Peta had glumly arrived at the same conclusion. They'd been warming up on the tennis court for ten minutes, waiting for others to appear for the round robin. Apparently the rest of the guests were giving it a miss this afternoon. Which left her alone with him if she wanted to stay and play.

"Care for a game of singles?" he asked, the eagerness in his voice a dead-set giveaway. He wanted to show her how good he was. Macho man strutting his stuff. In more ways than one, no doubt.

Peta wondered if the workout he'd give her on the tennis court was worth the aggravation of dealing with a come-on and decided it probably was. She was a bit stiff from the ride this morning. A good hard game of singles, followed by a swim in the heated indoor pool, then the warm relaxation of a hot spa tub, a light dinner, the meditation session with Thai monks... surely she'd sleep like the dead tonight.

"Okay," she agreed.

Predictably he started stripping off for the real action. The gentle warm-up ralleys had hardly been a test of skill, merely a stroking of the ball back and forth over the net. Peta watched him remove his tracksuit with cynical eyes, refusing to be impressed. She'd been fooled by physical attraction once too often. Never again, she fiercely vowed.

Not that he had Giorgio's lean elegance. Matt Davis was a much bigger man, his tall frame amply packed with muscle. However he did share the same air of ingrained self-assurance, quick to sum up an object of desire and confident it was within his grasp any time he cared to reach out. Peta had instantly been struck by it and subsequently goaded into an uncharacteristic show of defiant provocation... *Look all you want, Mister, but I'm not up for grabs!*

All the same, he did have a certain charismatic maleness that no woman could completely ignore. Strength, Peta decided, was his main asset. Matt Davis looked capable of standing up to anyone or anything. It wasn't just his powerful build, either. Peta sensed the kind of character that would take on any business and make a success of it.

He had a strong face, every feature carved with definition; a squarish, determined chin, a mouth full of straight white teeth, a nose that seemed to flare with passion, rather prominent cheekbones providing an emphatic underlining for surprisingly light grey eyes...very luminous and piercingly direct eyes shining from between rows of thick black lashes. Straight brows added to his no-nonsense look, as did the thick, closely cropped black hair.

Most people would see him as the solid, dependable type, but Peta wasn't about to trust that image. She'd seen and felt the simmer of sexual speculation emanating from him and no way was she about to fulfil the fantasies flying through *his* head. Giorgio was definitely the last man who would ever lead her down the garden path, whispering sweet nothings that came to precisely that. Nothing. From now on *she* was taking charge of her life and she was not going to have her judgment seduced by sex appeal.

"Speaking of singles…are you?" she asked, looking for feet of clay under the magnificent masculinity now revealed in navy shorts and a white sports shirt. His tan, she noted, was not of the sun-lamp variety. It had the natural glow of healthy outdoors activity. However, that did not preclude lots of indoor activity, as well.

He frowned incomprehension. "Pardon?"

"Single, unattached, on the loose?" she rolled out with a quizzical little smile. "I mean the wife could be taking a separate vacation while you do your filial duty. Or you might have an understanding lover sidelined until further notice…"

"No," he cut into her flippant little speech. "I'm not in a relationship at the moment. Haven't been for quite some time."

"Prefer to be fly-by-night, do you?" she tossed at him.

He hesitated. "Is that what you prefer?"

She arched her eyebrows and shook her head. "You shouldn't believe everything you hear about air hostesses and pilots."

"I was asking about you in particular."

"And I was asking about you. Some guys are take it and run specialists."

She heard the bitter edge on her voice and saw it give him pause for thought. She didn't care. If he was of that ilk, let him be warned the only thing he'd get from her was frustration.

"That's not my style. Though I guess there could be circumstances that might influence me," he answered slowly, his eyes sharply scanning hers.

"Well, it's my guess you do whatever suits you, Matt Davis. Like the salt and the cigarette," she said dryly.

And like Giorgio, keeping her on a string with a stack of cheating lies. Two years she'd wasted on him while he'd kept his real life hidden from her, holding out the promise of a future that was never going to happen. She'd hung on every flight to Rome, wild for the intense romance he showered on her, and all she'd been to him was a bit of fluff on the side.

She thought of her sister and the husband who adored her and their new baby and felt almost sick with envy. Why couldn't she meet a decent man who didn't shy clear of commitment? Just the mention of the word, *baby,* over lunch, had made Matt Davis bolt for a different tack in the conversation.

Her eyes flashed icy derision at the man who'd taken one look at her today and got bed on his brain.

"You want to know about me? I'll tell you straight before you start nursing any ideas of fun and games.

The next guy who wants to get in my pants will have to put a wedding ring on my finger first!''

His jaw visibly sagged.

Peta smiled. "Ready to play now?"

CHAPTER FOUR

A WEDDING ring?

She *wanted* marriage? Actively *wanted* it?

The tennis ball whizzed past Matt so fast he was left totally flat-footed, his racquet still balanced in both hands. Her first serve and she'd aced him!

He saluted her, graciously conceding her the point. She grinned, her face alight with triumphant pleasure at surprising him. Her jaunty walk to the other side of the service line gave warning this had not been a fluke shot. Peta Kelly could really play. Strong arm for a woman, too. Great coordination. He wished she would take her tracksuit off so he could watch her fantastic body in action. The baggy trousers and sweatshirt frustrated his...

The next ball shot down the centre line, leaving him standing again!

"Okay! So I've got the cannonball express on the other side of the net," he remarked appreciatively.

She laughed. "Should I slow up for you?"

"No. I've just got to adjust my pace a bit."

A lot, as it turned out. She was dynamite on the court. Not only could she hit the ball with considerable power, her tactical play was terrific, running him around, lobbing over his head, killing him with deft drop shots. He'd just managed to catch up with her

29

at three games each when she decided to strip off and his concentration was blown to pieces.

Underneath the tracksuit was one of those jazzy little aerobics outfits, stretch shorts and a midriff top in shiny lime green and lemon, very tart and spicy. She blitzed him for the rest of the set and Matt couldn't bring himself to care. People talked about poetry in motion. Her cute sexy bottom, her flashing, fabulous legs, and her bountiful bouncing breasts would have made the most illiterate man in the world wax lyrical.

"Had enough?" she asked sweetly, having trounced him six games to three.

Matt couldn't help blurting out what was on his mind. "Are you counting on a long celibate period or are you ready for marriage right now?"

It stunned her speechless for several seconds. They'd met at the net after the last point played and he could see her cornflower eyes glaze in disbelief at the up-front question. She recovered slowly, the glaze giving way to a mocking challenge.

"Given the right man, I'd marry him like a shot. The problem is in finding him. At my age, that's akin to finding a needle in a haystack. The best ones are already taken and the rest have other agendas."

A touch of bitterness there. Matt figured she'd been recently let down and was still hurting from it. "How old are you?"

She shrugged, uncaring what he thought of her. "I'm twenty-eight and the years are getting faster."

"Not so old that you're out of the race."

"My sister is twenty-six, married to a great guy, and she's just had her first baby. Right now I'm feeling very old, very alone, and totally depressed with life in general. A roll in the hay will not fix me up so don't bother thinking it. On the other hand, another set of tennis…"

"You've got it."

He grinned to himself as he headed down to the end of the court, ready to play again. He had her pegged now. She was using him as a whipping boy for the guy who'd punched out her self-esteem. Several things she'd said over lunch fell into place. Dying her hair had made her feel better. No one was going to take her for a blond bimbo anymore. Matt figured her last lover had done a real number on her, no doubt about it.

But she'd come out fighting.

Choosing such flamboyant colours for her hair was not only a rebellious statement but an aggressive one. She was showing plenty of aggression on the tennis court, too. As for riding a Ducati…Peta Kelly had a lot of guts. No way was she going to hide in a hole and lick her wounds. Her attitude reeked of thumbing her nose at the whole damned world.

Matt admired her for it. He'd always admired people who picked themselves off the floor and got on with life. He wished his mother would do it. With any luck, Peta Kelly might be a good influence on her. She might also be the needle in the haystack *he'd* been looking for.

The lust she stirred gathered an exhilarating edge

of excitement. He played particularly well in the second set of tennis, giving her the workout she wanted and enjoying every minute of it. Sweat made her even sexier. He could see her being very athletic in bed, not the passive type expecting him to do all the work. Making babies with her could be a real pleasure.

He won the set six games to three, matching her previous victory.

"Found your rhythm," she remarked dryly as they met again at the net.

"Feeling good," he agreed. "Are you ready to have a baby?"

"What?"

"Like your sister. You said she had a baby recently."

A sigh of exasperation. "She happens to be married. I don't think being a single parent is the best idea in the world."

"I couldn't agree more. Every kid needs a dad as well as a mum. But suppose you find your right man and he puts a wedding ring on your finger, would you be prepared to start a family straight away?"

"Yes, I would." Very emphatic.

"What about your career?"

"I'd give it up."

"Just like that?"

"It's only a job," she declared defiantly. "You serve a million people, clean up after them…what's so great about that? I'd rather serve my own children." She made a rueful grimace. "Though I could probably get work in airline administration if we needed the money. With the cost of living what it is, most families can only survive on a double income these days.''

''Wouldn't you miss the glamour of travel?''

A scornful look. ''Believe me! When you've been all the places I've been, what you want most is a place to call home. And all it entails.''

''Could become boring,'' he suggested.

She glared at him. ''I'd expect you to say that.''

''Why do you ride a Ducati if you'd like *boring?*''

Her eyes glittered. ''That bike is my baby. I talk to it and it responds to me. It doesn't know how to cheat, either.''

''Ah! A baby substitute.'' He smiled happily. ''You really do want them, don't you?''

''What's it to you?'' she demanded, her eyes narrowing in suspicion, probably anticipating he intended making fun of her.

''A fascinating point of view,'' he answered truthfully. ''Most of the women of my acquaintance seem to think kids would be a hell of a drag on them. Too big a commitment. Lifelong responsibility. No telling how much they'd mess up their other interests...''

''If you run with the fast crowd, what can you expect?'' she said sardonically.

He shrugged. ''Maybe you're right. *You* certainly represent a different slice of life.''

''You bet I do. As far as I'm concerned, family is the real world. The rest is fairy floss, here today, gone tomorrow.''

Matt found this philosophy highly encouraging.

Peta Kelly was not only a spunky fighter, she was a stayer in the family stakes. "So how many kids would you like to have?" he asked, getting down to the nitty-gritty.

"A whole brood of them," she tossed at him belligerently. Her chin went up and she marched over to the bench seat where she'd dropped her tracksuit. Having set her racquet aside, she began pulling on the baggy trousers, ruining the lime-lemon symphony for Matt.

"No more tennis today?"

"You got even. Isn't that enough for you?"

"I don't mind if you beat me. I enjoy playing with you."

"I've had enough." The sweatshirt completed the cover up. She turned to him with a forced little smile. "Thanks for the game."

"My pleasure." On many levels.

"It was good," she conceded, then picked up her racquet and headed for the gate.

Matt swiftly collected his own tracksuit, slung it over his shoulder, and joined her for the walk back to the main building, blithely ignoring her dismissal of him. He saw no reason for her not to be sociable until they had to part for their separate accommodation.

"Just for the record, what do you consider a brood?"

She huffed and slid him a glittering look. "Six," she said silkily.

Quite a number in this day and age. Rather daunting, in fact. Very expensive, too. Just as well he could afford a big house and whatever help might be required.

"Want to peel off now?" she asked.

"What?" The provocative question was highly surprising, coming after her reading him the riot act about getting into her pants.

She stopped, planting a hand on her hip as she surveyed him with derisive disbelief. "Why aren't you taking to your heels? I'm a broody hen. A homebody. Not your type. I don't care that you look like Tarzan. I'm totally deaf to the call of the wild. You haven't got a hope of changing my mind."

Right! She hadn't been asking him to strip. She expected him to be scared off by the prospect of having to handle six kids. He would have to show her he was a man of mettle.

"I can see now why you think twenty-eight is old," he said seriously. "If you want six kids, you'd need to get started on them straight away. Give yourself time to space them out a bit so you can enjoy them as individuals."

She threw up her hands, almost hitting herself with the tennis racquet. "Why are you persisting with this?" she cried in exasperation.

"I like to understand people."

"Well, I don't want six. I only said that to...to..."

"See how I'd react?" he helped.

"Yes."

"How many do you really want?"

"Four, if you must know. That would be the ideal." Her face drooped despondently as she looked

off into the distance. "But I guess I'd make do with
two if I had to. Probably lucky to have two, the way
I'm going."

"Never give up on a dream," Matt advised, thinking four was really a more manageable number. Two
boys and two girls would be just fine. A well-balanced
family.

She sighed and resumed walking.

Matt figured he needed to correct her impression of
him. The image of Tarzan was not to his liking.
Though he had to admit the idea of carrying Peta
Kelly off to a tree house and mating with her on the
spot had a very strong appeal. She stirred quite a few
primitive instincts. He'd like to punch out the guy
who'd soured her on men. On the other hand, he suspected violence would not win her approval.

"I'm not an apeman," he stated as a matter of fact.
"I'm actually quite civilised. My mother house-
trained me from a very young age. She'd vouch for
that if you asked her."

It earned a wisp of a smile. "You're really worried
about her, aren't you?"

"Yes. She took my father's death hard. It's been
almost two years now and she makes no effort to get
over it."

"She must have loved him very much."

He heard the sympathy in her voice and frowned.
Had she really loved the guy who'd done the dirty on
her? Matt didn't like that idea.

"Don't give my mother sympathy. It'll only make
her worse," he warned.

She glanced sharply at him. "You're a hard man."

"No. A practical one. Sympathy feeds her grief which she uses as an excuse to indulge herself in misery. And might I add, for your benefit, it's a futile waste of time nursing a broken heart over a guy who wasn't worth loving."

Her eyes whirled in confusion. "Your father wasn't worth loving?"

"*He* was. I meant the scumbag who cheated on you."

"Oh!" Resentment flared. "I'd take it kindly if you minded your own business, Matt Davis, and left me to mind my own."

"You make it my business when you put me on the same level as him."

"That's it!" She wheeled on him and stamped her foot. Her blue eyes were laser bolts, searing him with fury. "I don't have to take any more from you and I won't."

"I could be the father of your children," he said blandly.

"What?" The laser bolts lost direction.

"Might be your best chance."

Her mouth fell into a very sensual pout as she dragged in a deep breath. Matt was tempted to step forward and kiss her, get her mind moving on a positive path. He thought better of it, remembering the fierce stipulation of the wedding ring. He didn't want to scare her off. He threw in another persuader for good measure.

"I think four's an ideal number, too."

Her breath whooshed out. She backed away, wagging a finger at him. "You…are making a fool of me."

"Nope. Just being practical."

"I don't believe you."

"I've had a hard time finding a woman who wants to be a wife and mother."

"I'm not listening to this."

"Think about it."

"You just want to have sex with me."

"Can't have kids without doing it," he said cheerfully.

"You're a cheat!"

"I'll give up smoking but be damned if I'll give up salt."

"You stay right here until I'm inside and out of sight. I've had enough of you."

"Facing the truth is always difficult. Go on then. All I ask is you give it some thought."

"Don't worry. I'm not likely to forget this."

"Good!"

She turned and marched off towards the door into the gym. She looked great with her bottom stuck out and her shoulders thrust back, emphasising the highly feminine curve of her spine.

"See you at dinner," he called after her, feeling rather like the Big Bad Wolf who wanted to gobble up Little Red Riding Hood. Peta Kelly was the most stimulating woman he'd ever met. And the most delectable.

She didn't reply, didn't glance back. He didn't expect her to. She was in shock at the moment. But given time, the seeds he'd planted in her mind would start to grow. They had fertile ground. After all, he and she wanted the same thing. Any reasonable person would see that.

CHAPTER FIVE

ONCE Peta was lost to his view and the pleasure of watching her was at an end for the time being, Matt decided on a stroll around the grounds. Best not to run into Peta again for a while, even accidentally. She needed some space to get things in proper perspective. Dinner would come soon enough.

He pulled on his tracksuit and headed up towards the pine forest. From there he could descend to the garden in front of the cottage where he and his mother had adjoining rooms. It occurred to him, as he walked, it was imperative to find out how long Peta was staying at the health farm. Today was Tuesday. His week here was up on Friday though he could probably manage to extend the booking over the coming weekend. He'd talk to Reception about it.

Without any conscious thought, Matt drew the packet of cigarettes and lighter from his trouser pocket and actually had one of the death-sticks—as his mother called them—between his lips, ready to light up, when he realised what he was doing. Habit was an insidious thing.

One more couldn't hurt, he reasoned, but the image of scornful blue eyes suddenly made him squirm over the urge to indulge himself. Damn it! He'd said he'd stop smoking and he would. Giving Peta Kelly any cause to accuse him of cheating again would muddy the issues between them. Besides, if he was going to have kids, he had to do the right thing by them.

He took the cigarette out of his mouth, broke it open and scattered the tobacco on the ground. He destroyed the remaining ones in the packet in like manner, then shoved the resultant rubbish in his pocket for later disposal in a garbage bin. Temptation dealt with. Resolution affirmed. He walked on with a springier step, breathing in the pure air of virtue.

Back at the cottage, he took a long hot shower, washing his hair to ensure Peta could not smell any smoke on him. He gave his teeth a good brushing, too, rinsing out his mouth with the peppermint flavour of the toothpaste. After all, a kiss was just a kiss, not an assault on her underwear. If the opportunity presented itself and she was willing to try him out...Matt grinned to himself. He bet a kiss with her would be dynamite.

He changed into clean clothes; jeans, T-shirt, and the sweater his mother always commented on. It was grey with two broad stripes of red and royal blue across the chest and sleeves. If his mother thought it looked so great on him, Peta might, too. No harm in stacking the cards his way.

He wondered what Peta would wear to dinner. The bag she'd brought with her wasn't large, more the size of an overnighter. The thought made a visit to Reception even more pressing, though surely she'd be staying longer than one night.

He checked his watch as he left his room. His

mother's afternoon appointments for the Face'n'Feet treatment and manicure would be over by now. He knocked on her door. No reply. Probably having a cup of tea in the main lounge room, he decided, and headed straight for Reception.

"Hi!" He flashed his most appealing smile at the woman behind the desk. Her name tag read Sharon.

"What can I do for you, Mr. Davis?" she responded warmly.

"A matter of desperate need, Sharon. A Miss Peta Kelly checked in today. Can you tell me how long she's here for?"

She bridled. "We're not supposed to give out that information, Mr. Davis."

He put a rueful tilt into his smile. "As a concession for the only male around? I forgot to ask her myself and we had a cracking game of tennis this afternoon. Best partner I've had since I arrived. I was hoping she was staying until Friday, too."

"Well…since you're a suffering male, surrounded by the female gender, I'll look it up for you." She checked her book. "You're in luck, Mr. Davis. Miss Kelly took the Petite Pamper Package, Tuesday to Friday."

"Great!" He grinned and saluted her. "I owe you one, Sharon."

She laughed. "We're here to serve."

Aglow with satisfaction, Matt breezed into the lounge room in search of his mother. It was a friendly room. Deeply cushioned sofas and armchairs and footstools were spread around numerous coffee tables loaded with a variety of books and magazines. In one corner, a bench held all the provisions for a variety of herbal and ordinary teas. In another, a three thousand piece jigsaw puzzle was laid out on a table as an ongoing challenge for any guest to try their hand at it. A piano sat in a third, inviting anyone to play. Best of all was the massive fireplace at the end of the room where burning logs crackled a warm welcome.

Good room for a family, Matt thought, as he strolled through it. A sociable room. No television. He particularly liked the piano. He'd had a few piano lessons as a boy, until they got in the way of football training and other sports. He regretted giving it up. The electronic keyboard he'd bought in recent years gave him a lot of enjoyment, but if he acquired a big house, he'd get a piano. His kids would have fun banging on it, just as he had.

His mother was sitting close to the fire, looking down at her hands spread out in front of her and wriggling her fingers. Having seen Skye and Janelle perform this curious action, Matt knew the nail polish from the manicure wasn't dry yet. What did surprise him was the rather smugly admiring smile on his mother's face.

"Pretty colour on your nails, Mum," he remarked, drawing her attention to his presence.

She looked up, her eyes sparkling with pleasure. "It's called Perfect Peach. It does look nice against my skin tone, doesn't it? The manicurist said it would."

He lowered himself into the chair next to her, smil-

ing his approval. "You should buy it. Better still, go
and have a manicure every week."

"Yes. I think I will. She dipped my hands into a
wax bath and it's made them feel soft and silky, not
old at all."

This was good news. "You aren't old, Mum. No
reason to feel it, either," he pressed pointedly.

"I might try getting my hair coloured, too." She
held up her hands to assess them again. "Not as bright
as my nails, but something like this peachy shade. It
does suit my skin."

This was even better news, taking a positive interest
in her appearance. "Great idea!" Matt enthused. He
reminded himself to give his secretary a box of her
favourite Belgian chocolates. Her health farm idea
was turning out to be a winner, in more ways than
one.

"Oh! You've got your really classy sweater on."

"Mmmh…"

"Did you have a nice game of tennis with Peta,
dear?"

"Yes, I did. She's a top 'A' grade player. Almost
wiped me off the court."

His mother looked delighted. "How wonderful to
find someone who can match you. It's so important
to be able to play together. Your father and I…"

Matt switched off from the list of fond recollec-
tions, his mind wandering to the games he'd really
like to play with Peta Kelly.

"Where does she live?"

He snapped out of his fantasies. "Who?"

His mother sighed in vexation. "Peta."

"Haven't got a clue."

An exasperated roll of the eyes. "Where is she now?"

He shrugged his ignorance. "She went off on her own after our tennis match."

"I don't know where your mind is, Matt." Her tone was loaded with reproof. "You meet an extremely attractive woman. She's competent enough to hold a responsible job, athletic, obviously very bright, and the right age for you, too. It's opportunity handed to you on a plate and you just let it go past you."

"Oh, I wouldn't say that, Mum."

"You're not even trying." She turned away in disgust and stared bitterly at the log fire. "You'll end up a lonely old bachelor and I'll never get a grandchild."

How about four in fairly quick succession?

Matt didn't voice the thought.

Some things were best kept private.

His mother could be embarrassingly heavy-handed in her matchmaking efforts and he preferred to run his own race. Besides, he couldn't be certain of winning. He couldn't be certain it would turn out how he wanted it to with Peta Kelly. But he meant to give this chance a damned good try.

Driven by furious energy, Peta ploughed through twenty laps of the pool with barely a pause. Only when her chest started aching did she slow down and change to a leisurely sidestroke. Her mind, however, did not ease off its fuming activity. Matt Davis's poking and prying into her heart, followed by his outrageous advice with the focus on him as her future interest, still made her burn.

Devious, cocky man! Trying to turn her personal wounds to his own profitable advantage. He'd obviously taken her blunt honesty as a challenge and couldn't let it pass, worming out how best to get to her, then presenting himself as the answer to her dreams to be gratefully grabbed on the spot!

Peta knew what *he* wanted to grab. Did he think she was a fool who could be caught on the rebound if he held out a heap of glib promises? She ought to play him along and keep pinning him down just to teach him a salutory lesson. Yes…she would quite enjoy watching him wriggle on the hook he thought he'd baited for her.

Serve him right!

Except it would be a total waste of her time and energy. Better to ignore him. Though that would be rather difficult if he went along to the same activities she'd planned to enjoy here. His persistent presence could become an irritation, but she wasn't about to change her choices because of him. At least she didn't have to share the same table at meals. She could frustrate him on that score.

Peta hauled herself out of the water and dripped her way over to the wall switch that activated the hot spa pool. Having turned it on, she lowered herself into the bubbling warmth, finding a seat where the powerful jets hit her in all the right places. She needed to relax. It was counterproductive to her whole purpose in coming to the health farm to let Matt Davis work her into a lather.

The temper he'd raised gradually dwindled into a brooding gloom. It was a pity he wasn't Mr. Right. Physically he couldn't be faulted—a fine build of a man, obviously a good athlete, nothing objectionable about any of his features. Any woman would fancy a share of his genes for her children. High on intelligence, too.

As a stud, he could be considered almost perfect, but Peta didn't believe he was genuine about having fatherhood on his mind. No one came on that far that fast unless he was a con-artist. In fact, given the blatant sexual interest he'd already shown, his outrageous attempt to put marriage and children at the top of his list of wants was an insult to her intelligence.

Too much of an insult.

That afterthought clung, stirring niggling doubts over her angry dismissal of him as a candidate for Mr. Right. What if he had been frustrated in his search for a woman who wanted a family? Career women were holding off on motherhood these days. He'd certainly ascertained her attitude about her job before leaping in with his proposition of possibilities between them.

But he couldn't be serious...

No...it would be too much of a miracle if he turned out to be a really nice guy who wanted a family as much as she did.

The memory of last weekend with Megan and Rob and their baby brought a dull ache to her heart. Her sister was so lucky. Rob was besotted with his beautiful little son, supportive in every way. But it was baby Patrick who touched the deepest chords in Peta…holding him, cuddling him, smelling him.

Tears pricked her eyes. Damn Giorgio for fooling her into believing what couldn't be. Even now her mind writhed over the dreadful shock of seeing the photograph of his children…his…and his wife's.

She mustn't keep dwelling on it. She had to move on. Yet the need stirred by Megan's baby kept reminding her what she'd been cheated out of by Giorgio and his lies. It hurt. It hurt all the time.

She'd come to the health farm for distraction, for…

Maybe she should find out more about Matt Davis. The chance of him being sincere was highly remote but…why turn her back on a chance? She wasn't exactly inundated with eligible men and time was her enemy.

Even given the worst case scenario of his being a king rat, she was too wise to the seduction game to be taken in by ploys to bypass her wedding ring edict. At the very least he would provide some distraction from her misery over Giorgio.

Dinner tonight.

Avoiding him wouldn't achieve anything.

Though if Matt Davis thought he could make a meal of her, well, let him try. He would end up choking on the sweets course.

CHAPTER SIX

SEVEN o'clock at last! The guests in the lounge room started moving out for dinner. Others were coming down the stairs from the accommodation provided on the upper floor. Matt was starving, not only for food but for the sight of Peta Kelly again. He tried to hurry his mother in his eagerness to satisfy both needs.

She hung back. "You go on, dear. I think I'll visit the powder room first."

Matt sighed. No forethought. Since he might have missed seeing Peta on her way to the dining room, he didn't want to wait. "Okay, Mum. Don't be long."

He was at the door when he remembered he'd left the salt cellar in his tracksuit pocket. A quick scan of the women already in the dining room did not pick up the vibrant hair of Peta Kelly. Making a snap decision, Matt turned away and hotfooted it to the cottage. Dinner without salt could not be stomached. Five minutes at most it took him, yet on his return he found both his mother and Peta seated at the table, having a cosy chat.

Suspicion instantly hit. His mother could not have visited the powder room. She had deliberately held back to snaffle Peta Kelly and pursue her maternal matchmaking. Silently cursing the unwelcome interference in his affairs, Matt hastened to his chair.

The pleasure of seeing Peta in her red sweater again momentarily wiped out his disgruntlement at his mother's tactics. He smiled at her as he sat down, undeterred by the guarded look in her eyes. Peta Kelly was strong-minded enough to put his mother off if she hadn't wanted to sit with them. It was a good sign she was here. It meant she was prepared to explore the situation further.

"Peta went for a swim in the pool after tennis," came the first piece of personal digging from his mother. "She likes swimming."

"Mmmh…" said Matt, hoping his mother hadn't bragged about his swimming trophies from school carnivals. All the same, he was pleased to hear Peta enjoyed the same activities he did.

"And she leases an apartment with two other stewardesses at Bondi Junction," his mother smugly informed. "Peta was just telling me about having put in for a transfer to domestic airlines. She's seen enough of London and Rome."

"Well, I guess Australia is home," he commented happily.

It showed Peta was serious about settling down. Though her decision might have been triggered by the outcome of her last relationship. If her lover had been English or Italian, it could account for a wish never to revisit his stamping ground. Which was fine by Matt. It meant the guy couldn't come sniffing around her again, upsetting the applecart.

"Matt lives at Bondi Beach," his mother slid out,

obviously pleased with the short distance between their domiciles.

"Not with you, Cynthia?" Peta asked.

"Goodness, no! That wouldn't suit him at all."

Hard blue eyes flashed at him. "Why not?"

Her cynical thought was easily read... *Cramp your style?*

"Mum lives at Gosford on the central coast. My business requires me to be in Sydney," he answered matter-of-factly.

"And what business is that?" she inquired.

"Merchandising."

"Matt owns his own company," his mother rushed in. "It's very successful but it has taken up a lot of his time, working long hours with his wheeling and dealing. He hasn't stopped long enough to find himself a nice girl to settle down with. I keep telling him..."

Here it comes, Matt thought in exasperation, and cut in before the floodgates opened on the nagging subject of grandchildren. "I have made time for you, Mum," he reminded her.

She frowned at his interruption. "Yes, I know, dear. I'm not saying you haven't been good to me..."

"Ah! Stuffed mushrooms," he said with satisfaction as the waitress served them with starters. Dinner was always more to his taste than lunch. He got out the salt cellar and sprinkled away, then caught a crooked little smile playing on Peta's lips. He grinned openly at her. "I did tear up the last of my cigarettes."

It surprised her. Her eyes took on a wondering look.

"I'm so glad to hear that, Matt," his mother warmly approved.

"Well, there's always the village store if you get desperate," Peta said dryly, not ready to believe too much.

"No. The deed is done," he assured her and attacked his mushrooms with a hearty appetite.

The food shut his mother up for a while.

"What's the name of your company?" Peta asked as the plates were cleared away.

"Limelight Promotions," Matt answered, wondering if she intended checking up on him. It was obvious she wasn't taking much on faith anymore. He didn't blame her. Once burnt, twice shy.

"It's at Rockdale, just past Mascot Airport," his mother supplied brightly. "You'd both take the same road to work."

Matt gave her a baleful look. She just couldn't keep out of it.

Thankfully Peta ignored the comment, asking, "How do you manage the noise factor from the flights coming in?"

"The building is soundproofed."

"You'd need it," she commented.

"Oh, Matt spares no expense in looking after his employees," his mother gushed. "He's done very well. Very well, indeed. You might have read in the newspaper a little while ago about an apartment at Bondi selling for 1.2 million dollars?"

"Mum…" He was too late to stop her.

"It was Matt who bought it," she boasted.

The cornflower blue eyes widened and Matt had the sinking feeling they were propped open with dollar signs as they stared at him, probably calculating how much he was worth. He didn't want her to want him for his money. He hated this kind of boasting, hated how the knowledge of his wealth could affect people's opinion of him, their manner towards him, their assumptions about him.

"It's an investment," he said curtly. "I don't live in it. It's rented out to cover the loan from the bank. It's a matter of negative gearing…"

He clamped his mouth shut, stopping himself from explaining how he managed his finances. It wouldn't do any good. The damage was done. Her eyes had taken on a speculative look, no doubt seeing him as a far more attractive proposition than previously.

Funny…the question of money had never come into the equation of his relationships with Janelle and Skye. Janelle had been earning a six figure income from her legal practice. Skye was a high-flyer in the fashion industry, probably raking in a fortune of her own. Matt didn't know what an airline stewardess earned but it wouldn't be in that league.

Did the thought of snagging a millionaire excite her? Maybe she would now loosen up her underwear. The thought did not excite him. He much preferred Peta, the fighter.

"Excuse me. Dinner calls," he muttered, rising from the table to go to the hot buffet where the main course was laid out. Let his mother babble on if she had to. Suddenly he didn't care.

Barbecued chicken, boiled potato, broccoli, beans, grilled tomato with basil…not bad…except he'd somehow lost his appetite. Nevertheless, he heaped up his plate and returned to the table. A man had to eat. Peta and his mother and the others from the table had joined the queue to the buffet so he could salt his food without an eyebrow raised. Driven by a sense of discontent he almost drowned it in salt.

His garrulous mother and the tantalising red sweater returned to torment him again. Matt tried to concentrate his attention on the meal but his mind kept wandering. Maybe he was being oversensitive about the money issue. He wished it hadn't been brought up so soon, but there was no denying the advantages of being financially secure when it came to marriage. Peta had to see there was no problem about starting a family straight away. Of course, other important factors had to be weighed first. Like her attitude towards sex. Especially with him!

The two women chatted on about family. He learnt that Peta had two older brothers, John and Paul, as well as the younger sister, Megan, who'd just had a baby. Two boys, two girls…the same family she wanted. Her parents lived at Blackheath, up in the Blue Mountains, about two hours' journey from Sydney.

In turn, his mother explained Matt was an only child. She'd almost died having him, and his father wouldn't risk her trying for any more. Which was a shame, since there was only Matt to carry on the family line and provide her with grandchildren and he was now thirty-three and *still single*. Heavy sigh.

"I daresay you spoiled him terribly since he was your only child," Peta remarked sweetly.

Matt instantly recognised a dig at him. His gaze flew up. "I was not spoiled," he stated firmly before his mother could begin raving on about his childhood, indulging herself with a string of potentially embarrassing memories.

"He was always good-natured," she popped in, thankfully showing admirable restraint.

"My father set rules and he saw that I kept to them," Matt insisted, holding Peta's challenging gaze. "He taught me responsibility and I respected his lessons. I'd do the same with my own kids. *If* I ever have them," he added darkly, resenting her assumption he'd been a spoiled little rich kid.

"Then why do I have the impression you're used to getting your own way?" she inquired archly.

"Probably because I've *made* my own way," he retorted. He certainly hadn't had everything handed to him on a plate. His parents had been reasonably well off but they'd never had the kind of money he'd accumulated.

She smiled but it wasn't a smile of acceptance or approval. "So now you feel you can buy anything or anybody you want."

Her eyes said... *Not me, Mister. Not in a million years!*

He stared directly into the glittering derision,

fiercely willing her to back down from the insulting assumption she was making about him. Her gaze did not waver. Neither did the sparks of contempt. To Matt, it was like a punch in the guts, draining him of any lingering desire to win her over.

The accusation of being a cheat had some basis. It could be excused, even turned into a bit of fun between them. But not this. He didn't care where she was coming from or what some other man had done to her, she had no cause to think he used his money to get himself a woman. As though he couldn't attract anyone on his own merits!

"Actually, I have no taste for whores or gold-diggers," he drawled, mentally sliding sheets of steel between him and the woman who was bent on belittling him so meanly. His eyes returned her contempt and he had the brief, savage satisfaction of seeing *her* recoil from it.

"Matt!"

The shock in his mother's voice tapped at his social conscience. Polite behaviour should reign at the dinner table. "I'm sorry." He raised his eyebrows, inviting correction for the crass comment. "Did I misunderstand the implication in what you were saying about me, Peta?"

Her cheeks flooded with hot colour.

Good! If she wanted to fire arrows, let her burn from the sting of them!

"Perhaps I should have said I can't buy the kind of wife I want," he went on. "She'd have to want for herself, the same things I want out of marriage.

Otherwise it wouldn't work, and not all the money in the world could fix it."

Let her chew on that!

"Money does help though, Matt," his mother put in anxiously, worried by the tension in the air which was not at all conducive to the outcome she wanted from this encounter. "Financial problems often put a strain on a marriage. It's much better not having to worry."

Matt didn't need this advice. "What I *can* buy is property," he went on purposefully, wanting to ram the good intentions he'd been nursing down Peta Kelly's throat. "For example, I wouldn't have too much trouble finding the means to purchase a five bedroom home, with a pool and a tennis court thrown in. *If* I had a use for it."

The blue eyes went blank.

"*Five* bedrooms?" his mother queried, astonished at his choice. "Most modern homes don't have more than four."

Matt kept his gaze boring into Peta's, relentless in nailing his point. "I believe the question was buying power. Satisfied?"

She came out fighting, her cheeks still aflame but stubborn pride in her eyes. "Since you have so much to offer, perhaps you should draw up a premarriage agreement to protect yourself. It would avoid the risk of being taken to the cleaners by some unscrupulous woman…" she paused, baring her teeth "…should the marriage fail to live up to your expectations and you want a divorce."

"Oh, I so dislike that practice!" his mother declared, shaking her head in a pained fashion. "How can any marriage work without trust and real commitment? People shouldn't enter into it if they're already looking for it to fail."

"I couldn't agree more," Matt said emphatically, cutting Peta's feet out from under her.

She stared at him.

He stared right back, daring her to continue her attack on his character, promising her a retaliation she wouldn't forget. Confusion crept into her eyes. She dropped her gaze, giving up the fight.

To Matt it was a hollow victory. Nothing had been won. A sense of loss gnawed at his guts. He told himself he was better off not getting involved with Peta Kelly. Let her stew in her own sour juices. Shouldering her bitter baggage would bring him no happiness.

For once, his mother decided discretion was the better part of valour and didn't persist in pushing her opinions. Peta didn't offer any more. Ignoring the silence that had descended at their end of the table, Matt mechanically went through the process of finishing his meal. His stomach staged a mini-revolt but he kept forcing the food down, determined to eat the lot.

However, when his emptied plate was collected by the waitress, he simply couldn't face the sweets course which had been laid out on the buffet table. It was passionfruit mousse, an ironic reminder that the passion he'd fancied with Peta Kelly had been killed stone-dead.

His mother attempted to revive conversation, asking Peta what pampering she had decided upon and expounding on the pleasures of the treatments she had experienced here. Matt shut his ears. He decided to walk down to the village hotel and get roaring drunk. To hell with health!

"Are you going to come to the meditation session with the Thai monks, Matt?" his mother asked, tentatively reaching through his silence.

"No, I'm off for a walk in the clean night air," he answered, casting a mocking look at Peta Kelly as he rose from the table. "I hope the meditation will help you relax so you can sleep well. It would be a pity not to get some benefit out of coming here."

Before either of them could say a word, he flashed a smile and added, "Please excuse me, both of you."

He left without a backward glance.

What was dead was dead.

CHAPTER SEVEN

THE clean night air was decidedly chilly. Winter in the southern tablelands was more biting than in Sydney. Matt dropped into the cottage to don his parka and gloves. There was no point in freezing to death when all he wanted was a pleasantly pickled mind and body. Alcohol might not promote joie de vivre tonight but it should numb the pain of dashed hopes.

As he emerged from the cottage, his attention was drawn by running footsteps on the flagged terrace leading from Reception. His gaze narrowed on the flying figure of Peta Kelly. She caught sight of him and came to a panting halt, her eyes wildly targeting his, a sense of urgency pulsing from her. Matt's mind raced to account for it.

"Is there something wrong with my mother?" he shot at her.

"No!" She shook her head to allay any such fear. Her hands lifted in an agitated gesture of appeal. "I...I just wanted to catch you...speak to you..." She spoke jerkily, out of breath and totally discomposed.

Matt noticed she was now wearing her leather jacket, though she hadn't stopped to zip it up. Gloves were clutched in one hand. She'd obviously meant to run him down however far he'd gone. Which piqued his curiosity.

"Taking a risk, aren't you, Peta? Little Red Riding Hood chasing after the Big Bad Wolf?"

Her head jerked into an anguished little roll. "I'm sorry," she burst out. "I know you must think I'm not worth any more of your time, but...I really am sorry for what I said to you at dinner."

Sorry she'd wrecked a chance that might have been viable? Too late, lady, Matt thought grimly. Peta Kelly had shown her true colours and he didn't like them. He didn't want any part of them.

"We're all entitled to our own opinions," he said, dismissing her apology as unnecessary.

"Not if they're not fair," she retorted, her face pained by the admission.

It made him pause, frown, his own sense of fairness being pricked. Was she genuinely upset at her misjudgment of him or did she have another agenda?

"May I walk with you?" she pressed.

Cynicism instantly resurfaced. He was nobody's fool. If she thought she could sweeten him up and get the ball running between them again, she was in for a bout of frustration. Do her good, too. A return dose of her own medicine.

He shrugged carelessly. "It's a free country. Though if it's an escort you're wanting, I should warn you my goal is the local pub and I intend staying there quite a while." He wasn't about to put himself out for her. "And I don't give a damn if you call that cheating," he added, his eyes stabbing home his scorn for her opinion of him.

She took a deep breath and nodded. "Fair enough!"

Vexed by her emphasis on fairness, he strode out down the driveway, uncaring that she had to hasten her step to keep up with him. He hadn't invited her. He didn't want her tagging along, reminding him of the lust she'd stirred and the blind way he'd rushed in and suggested there might be a future for them. No doubt she was now wishing she hadn't killed off her options with him. He wasn't a bad catch, after all. Well, let her sleep with her regrets! He didn't need a woman who couldn't see straight.

"I truly am sorry for hurting you like that."

Her soft plea was like a bee sting to his pride. He stopped, glaring at her in the semidarkness. "I'm not bleeding," he bit out.

"I am," she answered quietly. "And I'm deeply ashamed for taking it out on you, Matt."

The sincerity coming from her was so strong, Matt couldn't quite bring himself to disbelieve it. "Want to explain that?" he said, cursing the impulse to invite more from her even as the words tripped off his tongue. There was nothing to be gained by prolonging this encounter. He should have just accepted her apology and let the whole issue between them drop.

She grimaced and resumed walking, head down as she pondered what to tell him, or mulled over whether telling him anything would do any good or not. Matt fell into step, slowing his pace to match hers. He could afford to show her a bit of consideration. Maybe she *was* bleeding.

"You were right this afternoon," she said on a rueful sigh. "I have been colouring you with my experience of someone else. You're rather like him in some ways."

Matt gritted his teeth, his pride stung again. Charming to hear he resembled some cheating bastard. Besides, whatever the likeness, it was no excuse to load him with crimes he hadn't committed.

"It's only been two weeks since I found out he'd been married all the time he'd been...attached to me. Two whole years of leading me to believe..." She caught her breath and released a long, ragged sigh. "Not only married, but with three children, as well," she added bitterly.

Two years? "How did he manage it?" Matt asked, forgetting to remain uninvolved, amazed that such a deception could be carried on so long.

"I met him in Rome. He was there on business. He actually lived in Milan but he always met me in Rome whenever I had a scheduled layover there."

"Convenient."

"Yes. And he'd have everything planned. It seemed...all he thought of was how to give me the most pleasure. Surprises. Romantic settings. Lovely gifts..."

"The perfect Latin lover," Matt remarked sardonically.

"He certainly played the part," she agreed. "He couldn't believe I'd walk away from what he offered when he finally confessed he had a wife and family. He thought he could buy my compliance to the situation, that I'd be happy to remain his bit on the side.''

The money angle. It must have stirred up painful memories and she'd lashed out indiscriminately. Nevertheless, it didn't excuse her for assuming he was bent the same way as her erstwhile lover. He was a different person. Though perhaps she didn't see that as clearly as she should.

''Am I a look-alike?''

''What?''

She seemed befuddled, as though he'd dragged her out of a deep mire of memories.

''You said I was like him in some ways,'' he reminded her.

She managed a wry smile. ''Not really. Not anymore. I guess you could call it a first impression. The way you sized me up and decided you wanted me. The air of confidence. It got to me.''

''Instant urge to slap me down, huh?''

''Something like that.''

Because she'd felt a tug of attraction and wasn't ready for it, distrusting feelings that had led her badly astray? Matt suddenly found it of urgent importance to ask, ''But I don't look like him physically?''

''Not at all.''

Relief flooded through him. She was not likely to confuse the two of them again. He really hated the idea of being taken for someone else, especially when the someone else was a double-dealing rat.

They'd already walked beyond the grounds of the

health farm and were heading down the road towards the village. Matt noted that the stars were very bright, no pollution to dim them out here in the country. The crisp air was invigorating. Getting drunk did not seem such a good idea anymore. Maybe there was a chance with Peta Kelly after all. *If* she could put the other guy behind her.

''Do you still love him?''

''No.'' Very emphatic. ''He didn't love me. He enjoyed having me.''

Disillusionment. It was a killer all right. At least she was seeing straight on the Latin lover. Not that Matt could blame the guy for wanting her. He himself had taken one look and…no doubt about it, he would enjoy having her. The question was…would she enjoy having him?

She'd stopped using him as a whipping boy. Her apology and confession surely meant she cared about his opinion of her. Or it could mean only that she didn't like herself for having stuck the knife in where it wasn't deserved. Best not to assume too much. She was trudging along beside him, head down, immersed in thoughts that probably had nothing to do with him.

They were approaching the outskirts of the village. Matt found himself riven with uncertainty, which was not a feeling he liked. Would she slap him down if he asked her to have a drink with him in the pub? Nothing risked, nothing gained, he told himself. Besides, now he understood where she was coming from, his pride could take another knock.

He was about to open his mouth when her steps

faltered to a halt. Her head lifted and jerked around as though she'd lost her bearings and needed to find them again. She stared at the streetlight up ahead then swung her face towards him. Her eyes glittered, but not with derision. Matt recognised the shiny wetness of tears, barely held in check.

"I'll go back now," she said huskily. "Thank you for…for listening to me."

"It's okay," he said, instinctively comforting. But damn it! It wasn't okay. He didn't want her swimming in a sea of misery over the bastard who'd deceived her. It wasn't the end of her dreams. She was so gut-achingly beautiful, desirable, her lips slightly atremble…

His heart kicked and civilised man disappeared under a rush of blood to his head. His whole body sprang alive with primitive urges as he stepped forward, wrapped Peta Kelly in his arms, and kissed her, kissed her with mind-pounding passion, wanting to wipe out the Latin lover from her life, wanting to stamp his own imprint on her, wanting a million things he couldn't stop to think about but *she* pulsed at the core of them.

Peta didn't know how it had happened. Her body was crushed against his, and his mouth was hotly bent on invading hers, and her head was whirling, the black depression that had settled in her mind attacked by a buzz of sensations, compelling her to do nothing but feel what he was doing to her.

Then his tongue was tangling with hers, tingling

over her palate, firing a wild eroticism that pulled her into responding, angrily at first because he was taking without her consent, but curiosity and the sudden surge of need to experience him drove her into plundering his mouth with all the passionate energy of wanting hurts to be salved, dreams to be restored, self-esteem mended.

And the power of the kiss streamed through her, healing, exciting, exhilarating, making her feel like a whole woman again, brilliantly, exultantly alive and pulsing with the pleasure of it. The cold, bleak sense of being alone and adrift was swept away in a tide of heat. She smouldered, burned and melted when a hand closed over her breast, gently kneading her inflamed flesh, a thumb brushing her nipple, making it extend, stiffen, beg for more attention.

Without any conscious realisation of what it was doing, her body sought the satisfaction of feeling his arousal, pressing closer, going up on tiptoe to cradle the thick, enticing bulge where it was needed. His mouth eased from hers and a groan swam into her ears as he adjusted his stance. It was not until he moved against her, actively accommodating what she had blindly initiated, that Peta came to her senses.

Shock slammed through her mind. She was encouraging an intimate connection with a man she barely knew, revelling in his kisses, his touch, his…manliness! Her hands were gripping his head and neck, fingers threaded through his hair, holding him to what he'd started, pressing for more. She'd lost all cognition of time, place, and circumstance.

Her heart kicked with fright at what she had unwittingly done. Her hands scrambled down to grasp hard, muscle-bound shoulders. She jerked her head back to disarm another lethal kiss and pushed some breathing distance between them.

"Stop," she gasped.

It jolted him into looking at her, though he seemed to have difficulty in focusing his eyes. The message was slow in filtering through his system but it did reach him. The hand on her breast suddenly stilled. His lower body straightened, easing back from hers.

"It's okay," he said gruffly. "I didn't set out to…umh…get in your pants." He plucked his hand from her breast. "You didn't say anything about your sweater."

"No. I…" She didn't know what to say, how to explain herself. She swallowed hard, feeling hopelessly choked up.

"It's okay," he asserted more strongly. His mouth started stretching into a smile. "It's fine. Great. Bloody marvellous!" The smile widened to a dazzling grin. "Let's get married."

"What?" she gasped.

"Married," he repeated with deep relish. "Pity we're not in Las Vegas. We could do it tonight."

"Are you mad?" Peta squeaked.

"Never been saner in my life."

"Just to get in my pants?" Her voice reached a higher register.

"Nope. Going to have four kids, too."

Peta stared at him, completely dumbfounded. He

bent and scooped their gloves off the ground where they had somehow dropped. Then he took her limp hand, threading his fingers through hers and gently squeezing his strength into them.

"Come on. We'll unwind over a drink at the pub and make whatever plans you'd like for the wedding."

"Wedding," she repeated dazedly.

"It'd be much less fuss, probably quicker, too, getting married in a register office, but I know women like weddings. I wouldn't do you out of one."

He pulled her along with him and she let him.

Her mind told her it was utter madness.

She should go back to the health farm and try to sort herself out because she seemed to be in a helpless muddle. But he held her hand, pouring an irresistible energy into it, and her body had a will of its own. It wanted to go with him. It did.

CHAPTER EIGHT

DYNAMITE! No doubt about it, Matt thought exultantly, his body still zinging from the explosion of sensation. He was on Cloud Nine as he walked Peta Kelly to the village pub, amazed that he'd reached the age of thirty-three and never felt like this before, so incredibly, exuberantly alive and bursting with anticipation for more and more of the woman walking beside him, her hand snugly held in his.

He'd never really believed his father's tale of meeting Matt's mother and deciding to marry her on the very same day. Too simple, he'd thought dismissively, even cynically. It was undoubtedly a romantic rendering of the past. Marriage was too serious a business to decide upon so quickly. But he now understood how it could happen. All the right bells were ringing, telling him unequivocally that Peta Kelly was the one woman who'd make his life complete.

Thank God both Skye and Janelle had gone on their way, leaving him waiting for this! Not that he'd ever actually proposed marriage to either of them, just skirted around the subject, thinking of it as a possible extension of their relationship, more a rational playing with the idea—weighing pros and cons—than a compulsive desire to hold on to them forever. Nevertheless, he might have made a big mistake with either one of them and never known this feeling, this nerve-tingling sense of absolute rightness.

Peta Kelly was *the one*, just as his mother had been for his father. She might think it was a crazy impulse, proposing marriage out of nowhere, so to speak, but Matt knew he wasn't crazy. Many times in business situations, the right bells had rung for him, telling him to grasp the opportunity, ride the wave, pursue a certain course. It had happened with key employees, too, some extra sense insisting this person would do the job better than any other. Matt had learnt never to ignore his instincts. Much of his company's success had ridden on them.

No way was he about to ignore them now.

He wasn't crazy. He'd been absorbing everything about Peta all day, unable to think of anything else. The Latin lover had muddied their intercourse but that had been dealt with. Matt was confident they could go forward now. Peta was with him. She hadn't slapped him down or walked away. She was still with him. He hoped it meant what he wanted it to mean.

They entered the pub. Matt had forgotten how cold it was outside until warm air enveloped them, drawing them into the cosy atmosphere engendered by a huge log fire. He ushered Peta to a table near the friendly heat and saw her seated, reluctantly releasing her hand.

"What will you have?" he asked.

Her eyes looked huge and slightly vacant. Matt hoped she was overwhelmed by the same feelings coursing through him. It was difficult to concentrate on anything else.

"Beer, brandy, gin..." he helped.

"Yes. Gin. And tonic," she decided somewhat vaguely.

"Won't be a minute," he promised.

Matt strode to the bar, eager to get served and back to Peta as fast as he could. Fortunately the pub was fairly quiet and the bartender immediately obliged him. He ordered two gin and tonics since beer on his breath might not be desirable in these promising circumstances.

As the drinks were poured Matt eyed his surroundings with rather wry appreciation. Not exactly the place he would normally envisage for a marriage proposal, but probably no one would consider his proposal normal. He knew it was right for him. Somehow he had to make it right for Peta, too. And very possibly, this fine old country pub added a down-to-earth normality that would help his cause.

He liked the time-honoured features of the place—no temporary plastic furniture or throwaway posters—lots of old polished wood and brass, stained glass in the windows, historic photographs on the walls, mellow lamps, some quite impressive antique pieces giving a sense of lasting solidity.

It was what Matt wanted in a marriage...lasting solidity. Like his parents. Until death do us part. Though he hoped he wouldn't die as young as his father had. Only fifty-eight.

Just as well he'd decided to stop smoking today. A

family man had responsibilities, not least of which was to take care of himself so he'd be around for as long as a father was needed by his kids. Given four children, reasonably spaced, the youngest would only be eighteen when he was fifty-eight. Clearly there was no time to be wasted in getting Peta to agree to their marriage.

Seize the day, Matt thought as he paid the bartender, then picked up their glasses and headed back to the woman he wanted as his wife. His hormones had steered him absolutely right in driving him to seize her on the way here. It had resolved everything in his mind. In fact, he could hardly wait to seize her again. The walk back to the health farm loomed as a highly desirable exercise.

Peta seemed to be lost in some private reverie, unaware of anything around her. "Your gin and tonic," he said, planting the drink firmly on the table in front of her. It jolted her into focusing her eyes on him. She stared, as though seeing him for the first time and finding him worthy of close study.

Matt took the chair opposite hers at the table, careful not to crowd her and wanting her in his direct line of vision. Easy eye contact helped for positive persuasion. There was obviously much going on in her mind and he wasn't sure she was as convinced as he about their having a future together. He was used to making hard and fast decisions. Her judgment might be clouded by the mistake she'd made over the guy in Rome.

He smiled, projecting warm encouragement and approval. "I'm glad we got that sorted out."

She shook her head, her expression turning wary. "I don't think we've sorted out anything."

Obviously some positive thinking had to be stimulated. "Of course we have," Matt assured her, then ticked the points off on his fingers for her. "I'm not like your Latin lover. I'm an eligible bachelor with the best of intentions. We're extremely well suited. We're both ready to get married and start a family. There are no impediments to doing precisely that and the sooner we do it the better."

He could have added he had never been so sexually aroused by any other woman and he was envisaging an exciting length of time where she wore no pants at all, but he thought logic might work better for him at this point. He would reinforce the passion between them later.

"But I don't love you," she said, her beautiful blue eyes wavering under the certainty he was beaming at her.

Love... Matt's thought pattern was severely jolted, the emotional pull of that one word disrupting his straight-line plan of action.

What was love anyway? Something that grew out of passion, liking, respect. It would happen, he told himself. Besides, love didn't guarantee a future together. Her own experience should be telling her that. Where had love got her in the very recent past? Down the drain!

She needed some guidance on the more practical

aspects of marriage—the *real* living together, not the hearts and flowers stuff which was ephemeral anyway. If she'd been actually living in Rome she wouldn't have been fooled for so long.

"*'With my body, I thee wed,'*" he quoted at her, "and we've sure got the right chemistry for that to be a mutual pleasure. No denying the spark's there. We've got plenty to build on, Peta."

Hot colour shot into her cheeks, giving them a glow that rivalled the brilliant shine of her hair. Her eyelashes fluttered down. She picked up her drink. "I don't think that's enough to build a marriage on," she muttered and took temporary refuge in sipping the gin and tonic.

"You're right. Goodwill and mutual goals and a sense of commitment are more important," he said emphatically. "Half the world does very well with arranged marriages where such things are established beforehand. Love doesn't enter into them at all."

"I hardly know you," she cried, her inner agitation showing as she swirled her drinking straw around the ice cubes in her glass.

"Did you know the man who deceived you for two years?" he countered and instantly regretted the words as pain flashed across her face. Damn it! He didn't want to remind her of *him*, though she did need to appreciate knowledge came in provable facts, not just feelings. He'd already totted up in his mind quite a résumé on her life and background, just as she should have done on him by now.

"Peta...this can be a clean slate for both of us,"

he pressed gently, wanting to mitigate the hurt.
"There's no need to bring bad emotional baggage
from the past into the future we make for ourselves.
We care about the same things. We can share them."

It caught her attention. She was with him again.

Eager to appease her doubts and fears, he asked,
"What do you need to know?" willing to supply her
with any information she required in coming to view
a future with him more favourably.

His life was a fairly open book, no skeletons to
worry about. His secretary could probably list a few
faults but he wouldn't be human if he didn't have
some. Skye and Janelle could undoubtedly list a few
more—women being women. However, all relationships worked on give and take and compromise.
Marriage was no different. It was just longer on commitment.

The ice cubes clinked continually as Peta considered the need-to-know question. Matt didn't hurry her.
Assessing him in the light of a possible husband was
probably a big step for her and needed appropriate
consideration. Fortunately, the groundwork had already been laid. He couldn't be dismissed as an in-
adequate breadwinner. His health was good. They had
similar values, much in common, and their wedding
night shouldn't hold any fears, not after that kiss.

Her gaze shifted, fastening on his hands, one curled
lightly around his glass, the other resting on the table
near it. Was she remembering his touch on her breast,
the way she'd responded? He sat very still, not wanting to distract her, conscious of his own pulse picking

up tempo as erotic images played through his mind. Peta Kelly had the sexiest body he'd ever felt. And her mouth... As though her thoughts were attuned to his, her lashes lifted enough for her to focus on *his* mouth.

Matt was glad of the cover given him by the table. His heart pumped so hard it sent a rush of stirring blood to his groin. Keeping still was almost beyond him. He curled both hands tightly around his glass to stop himself from reaching out to her. The urge to leap up and haul her into his embrace again was close to irresistible.

"What you're putting to me..." she said slowly, her gaze lifting, sharply concentrated now as her eyes scanned his, "...is a marriage of convenience."

"Yes. Why not?" If she wanted to think of it like that, Matt didn't mind, as long as she was thinking of them being together. "Save us both from wasting more time," he pointed out, hunting for backup arguments. "I don't want to be an old dad. And I can't imagine anyone I'd like more as the mother of my children. Fine genes," he added for good measure.

It drew a wry smile. "Yours don't look so bad, either."

He grinned. "Consider me a sperm bank."

She sighed. "It's not that simple, is it? There is the matter of living together."

"Reasonable people can always find a way," he argued. Caring hearts also helped, he thought. Peta no more liked to hurt people than he did. The sense of fairness that had driven her to come after him tonight was very heartening. He could deal with that.

"And for all you seem very virile, you might fire blanks."

"What?"

"Have you fathered any children?"

Matt recovered from the shock of having his potency doubted. "I'm not an irresponsible sower of oats," he declared strongly.

She shrugged. "Just checking. If we should enter a marriage for the purpose of having children..."

"Okay. We'll have tests done first. Sensible idea," he approved, though he didn't feel like being sensible where Peta Kelly was concerned. He didn't want her to back out. There would be no reason to, he swiftly assured himself. His father had certainly sired him. Why shouldn't he be successful in the paternity stakes?

"I don't suppose you can ever be really sure," she mused. "Some couples try for years to have a baby..."

"That won't happen to us," Matt cut in decisively. Some guys had a low sex drive. He certainly wasn't one of them. With Peta, he'd have no problem working overtime on getting her pregnant.

She recognised the simmering gleam in his eyes and laughed self-consciously. "It's crazy even talking about this."

"It makes sense to me," he insisted.

She frowned, sipped more of her drink, then shook her head. "We only met today."

"How long does it take to recognise a great chance?"

Her eyes flirted uncertainly with his. "I couldn't marry you without a prenuptial agreement."

It was Matt's turn to frown. Money...divorce...he recoiled from both of those subjects. Surely with her background—parents still married to each other—she'd work at the same kind of lasting power. Or weren't her parents happy together? Good example or bad example?

Suddenly aware he didn't have knowledge he needed, Matt simply asked, "What do you want in it?"

"That if we don't have children, I have no claim on any property I didn't bring into the marriage." She leaned forward, pressing an appeal for understanding. "I'm not a gold-digger, Matt. If we got divorced, I wouldn't try to take you for..."

"Fine!" he agreed, pleased with her strong sense of integrity. The money issue was definitely dead and a childless marriage would be reason for divorce. Even churches granted annulments on those grounds. Matt had no hesitation in saying, "If that will make you feel better, we'll do it." Besides, he'd have Peta pregnant so fast, the prenuptial agreement would be null and void almost as soon as it was signed.

She sat back, relieved. A little smile began playing on her lips. "You really want four children?" she asked, the possibility of her dreams being answered pushing eagerness through caution.

"Yes, I do." He couldn't help smiling, relief and

triumph soaring through him. "I'm sure I'd be a great dad, too."

She laughed, then retreated again in confusion at her response to him. "This has to be pie in the sky."

Matt reached across the table and seized her left hand, his thumb deliberately marking the third finger. "I could buy you an engagement ring tomorrow. Would that make it real to you?"

She looked wonderingly at him, realising he was serious about it and unsure how to take it or what to do. Matt took great encouragement from the fact she didn't try to withdraw her hand. He held on to it, his fingers grazing across her soft palm, loving the touch of her skin.

"Pretend for now it is pie in the sky," he suggested. "Given that the law requires us to wait a month before we can get married, tell me how you'd like to proceed. Do you favour a diamond engagement ring? A sapphire to match your eyes? What kind of wedding would you like? Where would you like to go on your honeymoon?"

"Matt…" She was about to protest.

"Go on. Just for fun. No harm in talking."

She sighed, venting tension. "Just for fun then," she agreed.

Matt worked hard at making it fun as he drew her out on her dreams. He wanted Peta Kelly. He was going to win her. If he couldn't bulldose her into marriage, he'd seduce her into it, one way or another.

CHAPTER NINE

"Six days," Megan muttered, pausing her eyebrow pencilling to shoot Peta a beetling frown. "You can't be serious. It's crazy to think of marrying a guy you met only six days ago."

Peta lifted her gaze from the baby she was rocking in her arms and met her sister's incredulous glare in the mirror with a serene little smile. "Tell me that after you meet him today."

Matt had no qualms about confronting her family en masse at Patrick's christening which was only two hours away now. A man who ran a successful company was used to tricky meetings. Peta had little doubt he would dazzle her family into thinking anything was possible with him. His innate confidence had a power that even she had found irresistible.

Megan swung around, too disturbed to continue her makeup for the big family event. "You can't fool me, Peta. You've been doing crazy things ever since you came home from Rome. The hair, the bike... This getting engaged to Matt Davis is a rebound thing from Giorgio."

"You're wrong. It's the sanest decision I've ever made."

"Which makes my point." Megan's eyes jabbed at Peta accusingly. "You don't *love* him."

Her heart gave a sickening lurch and she swiftly dropped her gaze to the beautiful bundle of innocence she cradled close to her breasts. He'd fallen asleep and looked blissfully content. If all went well, within a year she'd have her own baby to hold and love and cherish. And she knew the love would be returned, a love that came with absolute trust. It was enough for her. She'd make it enough. She'd have her children and Matt would make a fine father. The painful emptiness she felt now would be filled many times over.

"Not everyone hits the jackpot, Megan," she said, struggling to hide the desolate core inside her. She lifted hard, defiant eyes to her sister. "I like Matt. He makes me laugh. Maybe laughter's worth more than love."

"Does he know?" Megan's concern sharpened. "You're not fooling him into thinking..."

"I'm not fooling him about anything. We understand each other very well. Matt wants children, too."

Megan shook her head. "There must be something wrong with him."

"Why?"

'Proposing a marriage like this. And so fast. Is he homosexual?"

"What?"

The shock of the question propelled Peta into a wild peal of laughter.

"It isn't a joke," her sister said furiously. "I'm really worried about what you're letting yourself in for. What if he only wants you to give him a family?''

"Believe me..." Peta choked out "...he wants me for more than that. Matt is very, very heterosexual.''

"Have you done it with him?"

Peta instantly sobered. "No, I haven't. And I won't. Not until we're married. I'll deliver when he delivers. I'm not going to be taken for a ride again, Megan.''

"For God's sake! You're making him pay for your own mistake. If you can't let Giorgio go, you're going to have one hell of a marriage.''

Peta's chin came up in fighting mode. "People used to wait for their wedding night. In many countries they still do.''

"Do you *want* him? I mean does Matt Davis turn you on sexually or do you intend to suffer him for the sake of having children?" Megan flung at her.

Heat flooded up her neck. "Not that it's any of your business...''

"Someone has to make you see sense!''

"...I won't mind sharing a bed with him.''

"*Mind!* If he's so very heterosexual, do you think he's going to appreciate lukewarm lovemaking? Let me tell you...''

"Okay! He turns me on," Peta cried in exasperation. "He's loaded with sex appeal. Satisfied?''

"Well, at least you've got one thing right," Megan muttered and swung back to the vanity mirror.

Peta simmered with resentment. She and Matt had this marriage all worked out. It was no one else's business but theirs. She'd come here to help Megan get ready for the christening and the family luncheon afterwards and her sister thought she had free licence to criticise—her *younger* sister who'd had everything fall beautifully in her lap. It was fine for her, sitting on her pedestal of perfection, everything laid at her feet...

"I'll get Patrick's bath ready while you finish your makeup," she said, walking quickly from the bathroom, ashamed of the rush of envy. She knew her sister spoke out of caring for her. It was just... Megan didn't understand. Couldn't. Her life had been different. And Peta didn't want to talk about it.

Rob was out on the patio setting up the barbecue for later. He'd probably been told to keep out of the way so Megan could have a heart-to-heart with her off-the-rails sister. Peta strode through the family room, hoping not to draw his attention through the glass frontage to the outdoors area.

She reached the nursery without incident and paused to admire it all over again. Megan had created such a delightful room for her baby, all apple green and white, wonderful mobiles hanging from the ceiling, pretty wallpaper with a border of bunny rabbits, colourful soft toys filling the shelves. Assuring herself *she* would soon be furnishing a nursery, Peta gently laid Patrick in his bassinette. He was still fast asleep. It was impossible to resist touching his face, running her fingertips lightly over the baby-soft skin.

Taking a deep breath to relieve the tightness in her chest, Peta stepped over to the change table to collect the baby oil and talcum powder for his bath. Megan had already laid out the christening robes which had been used for each newborn child in the family since their eldest brother had worn them for the first time. Peta stroked the exquisite silk and lace layette with a sense of reverence for each new life it had adorned.

Next year, she thought. Next year my mother will bring these clothes to me for my baby. Mine and Matt's. And by then I will have forgotten all about Giorgio and what he took from me because my life will be filled with love again. True love...

His mother stunned Matt by bursting into tears just as he'd picked up his car keys, ready to leave.

"It's my fault," she cried, wringing her hands in despairing anguish. "I know it's my fault. If I hadn't nagged you about a grandchild..."

"Mum!" He banged the keys down on the kitchen counter in sheer exasperation. "I've heard enough of this ridiculous nonsense. Will you get it through your head I'm doing what I want to do? It has nothing to do with you!"

"I pushed you together and now she's marrying you for your money," she wailed.

"Well, thanks a lot, Mum. I thought I had other things going for me." Sarcasm, he knew, was not becoming, but he was being pushed to the limit here.

"I'll go out more. I'll join clubs." Her voice rose hysterically. "I'll go on a diet and look after myself. You needn't worry about me. I can make a life without any grandchildren."

"Good!"

"So you don't have to get married and…"

"I want to marry Peta Kelly and nothing you say is going to stop me, so you might as well accept it, Mum. I told you…it's just like Dad with you…"

"Your father didn't move this fast. Six days…it was six months before he proposed. He courted me. He did things properly. And I loved him…"

His chest went tight. So Peta didn't love him. They'd settled on an arrangement. It would work. They wanted each other. It was enough. He dragged in a deep breath and released it on a sigh of determined finality.

"I have to go. I'll be late for the christening if I don't leave now. I'm sorry you're upset, Mum, but I assure you, there's no reason to be. Peta is not— absolutely not—marrying me for my money. Now please…" He tried an appealing smile. "…Just wish me well and let me go."

"Why do you have to rush into it?"

Because nothing was going to change and celibacy didn't suit him. Not where Peta Kelly was concerned. Unfortunately, he didn't think his mother would appreciate that point.

"Mum…I'm going. You've got six weeks to the

wedding if you want to start dieting. I would like the mother of the groom to turn up.''

He regathered his keys and headed for the front door.

''I can't approve of this, Matt,'' she called after him.

He paused at the door to look back at her. ''It's my life, Mum,'' he said quietly. ''My choice…my life.''

He left her on that note, thinking she would change her tune by this time next year. Once she had a grandchild to dote over, she would forgive and forget everything that had worried her.

A baby… Matt smiled to himself as he settled into his car for the trip back to Sydney. It would be great having a baby with Peta. It would bond them together as nothing else could.

As for love…

It would come.

It had to.

The feelings he had wouldn't make sense otherwise.

The build-up of tension eased the moment Peta saw Matt's forest green Jaguar turn into the church grounds. Her nerves stopped screaming. She could relax. He'd come. He wasn't even late. Her family had arrived early, eager for a get-together before the christening ceremony began, and their curiosity about the new man in her life had forced her to field a lot of awkward questions.

"There's Matt now," she said, hoping the words sounded more like delight than relief.

"He drives a Jag?" Her brother, John, was clearly impressed.

"What did you say he does for a living?" Paul inquired, the classy car having put his mind in sharper focus.

"Matt owns and runs a merchandising company. It's called Limelight Promotions," Peta answered with exaggerated patience.

"Guess he's used to getting what he wants when he wants it," John reasoned.

Peta glared at him. "I am not marrying Matt for his money."

Though she was glad he had it. As his mother said, it was much easier establishing a home and bringing up a family if there were no financial worries. Peta wanted the best for her children.

The Jaguar came to a halt in a parking slot. The driver's door opened and Matt stepped out, looking even more impressive than his car, his splendid physique enhanced by a perfectly tailored navy blue suit and everything about him shouting top executive class.

"Oh! What a handsome man!" her mother exclaimed, surprised and pleased.

"Definitely loaded with sex appeal," Megan muttered.

Yes, he was. He really was, Peta thought, a little thrill of anticipation tingling through her. "Excuse me," she said, and moved to meet him.

It would be all right…this marriage, she told herself fiercely. Any woman would be proud to have Matt Davis as her husband. And the sex would be good. No doubt about that. Best of all, he would give her the family she wanted because he wanted it, too.

A smile grew, lighting up her face and warming her soul as she walked towards the man who would be the father of her children.

Matt waited by the car, watching her come to him, too entranced to move forward himself. His chest felt as though it was fit to burst. She glowed. She outshone the rest of the world. Her smile sent tingles all the way to his toes. She was exotic and beautiful and everything he wanted in a woman. And she was his. Or soon would be.

The royal blue suit she wore moulded her curves with a sexy emphasis that had Matt fighting to control himself. The short skirt had temptation roaring through his head. Her long, lovely legs, shimmering in sheer black stockings, filled his mind with wildly erotic images. He wanted her so badly, it was all he could do to remind himself her family was watching and he didn't have Peta to himself. Yet.

"Hi!" she said, her eyes warmly welcoming him.

"Are you okay?" he asked, nodding to her family, trying desperately to focus on what was important today.

Her smile turned wry. "I hope you're up to an inquisition."

He grinned. "Man of steel."

It made her laugh. She had a lovely laugh, an infectious bubbly sound that seemed to dance through his heart. Matt looked forward to listening to it all his life.

"Maybe this will help," he said, drawing the small velvet box from his trouser pocket.

She stared down at it as he handed it to her. Her fingers fumbled over opening it. The diamond ring seemed to mesmerise her. She didn't exclaim over it. She didn't move to put it on. She stood utterly still, and to Matt's sharply scanning eyes, the colour drained out of her vivid face, leaving it oddly lifeless.

Alarm bells clamoured in his mind. Was the reality of their decision striking home to her? Would she back off, faced with this symbol of commitment? His whole being screamed to hold on to her. He acted, plucking the ring from its satin bed, taking her left hand in his.

"Allow me," he said gruffly, determined on sealing their agreement.

The magnificent solitaire diamond winked mockingly at her. It felt as though a vice had clamped around her heart, squeezing it unmercifully. It should have been Giorgio giving her this. She'd dreamed of it so many times… Giorgio, taking her hand, sliding on his ring…

It was wrong…letting Matt Davis do it.

I can't go through with this. I can't…

But if I don't...

Diamonds are forever...like children...solid, lasting dreams that could come true...

The ring settled into place.

Peta took a deep breath and looked up at the man who'd put it there, the man whose promises weren't empty, the man who wanted to stand by her, support her, whose strength she could lean on in the years ahead when they had their family.

"I'll be a good wife to you, Matt," she whispered.

Tears filming her eyes. Did a ring mean so much? Matt didn't understand. But he felt her giving herself to him and he forgot they were being watched by her family. Only she existed for him. He lifted her hands to his shoulders, wrapped his arms around her waist, and did what he needed to do.

He kissed her.

The apprehension that had seized him was swept away by an intoxicating rush of passion, flowing as fiercely from Peta as it did from him, and Matt exulted in it, loving the way her mouth responded to his, loving the feel of her body sinking against him, her wonderful soft breasts, her stomach, her thighs...his woman.

"Matt..." A feathering gasp against his lips, intensely sensual.

"Mmh..." Excitement pulsing through him.

"My family..."

A jolt of recollection. Matt struggled out of his

absorption in the sensations Peta aroused in him, opening his eyes to the embarrassed appeal in hers. Her cheeks bloomed with colour. She was vibrantly alive now and his heart soared with the pleasure of it.

"You've got lipstick on your mouth," she said dazedly.

He let her slide away from him and plucked the handkerchief from his breast pocket. "Better clean me up then," he invited.

She took the cloth and quickly erased the mark of their kiss. He didn't care. He could still feel it.

"Is mine smudged?" she asked anxiously.

"No." He grinned with pure happiness. "You look perfect."

She gave a self-conscious laugh and tucked his handkerchief back in his pocket. "They're waiting to meet you."

"And I'm all primed to meet them."

Another delightful bubble of laughter.

Matt caught her hand—the left one, wearing his ring—linking himself to her as they moved as one to begin facing the future together.

Megan watched their approach, ignoring the buzz of comment from the family as she keenly observed the man who had persuaded her sister to recklessly throw her lot in with him. She wanted to find fault. She wanted some cause to show Peta how wrong she was in entering a loveless marriage. Instead she found herself helplessly torn by what she saw.

He adored her.

That obvious truth kept echoing through Megan's mind, while festering behind it was the knowledge that Peta didn't love him. What would that do to him in the long run when his love wasn't answered by love, when the cup of hope was drained and disillusionment set in, emptying his heart of all the feelings beaming from him today?

It was wrong...wrong...

Yet what could she do?

She loved her sister and wanted the best for her.

Maybe Matt Davis was best for her.

Except...was it fair to him?

CHAPTER TEN

MATT glanced at his watch again. Only a minute had gone by since he'd last checked. It felt like a million years and there were still another four minutes to go.

His best man leaned over and dryly remarked, "If you're counting on punctuality, Matt, forget it. Brides are always late."

He managed a rueful smile at his old friend. A bank of good memories lay between him and Tony Beaman, a long sharing, yet he couldn't confide the uncertainties racking him during this wait. "That's true," he acknowledged.

True of the weddings he'd attended over recent years. He shouldn't be counting on Peta turning up at exactly eleven o'clock, but if she didn't, this unshakable anxiety was going to get a hell of a lot worse.

She'd been so quiet, withdrawn inside herself at the rehearsal on Thursday night and he hadn't seen her since. Though she had sounded all right on the telephone when he'd called, calm and full of organisational details for the wedding. He didn't really believe she'd get cold feet at this late hour. He just…*needed* her here with him.

A tap on his shoulder. He swung around to his mother who sat in the pew directly behind him, looking positively resplendent in a flowing peach outfit, her hair glowingly dyed a similar shade and lightened with artful blond streaks.

"I must say they've done a wonderful job with the flowers," she whispered. "The church looks lovely."

Flowers? Matt hadn't even noticed them. He did, however, hear the concession in his mother's voice and it wasn't a grudging one. Had she finally resigned herself to the inevitable?

"*You* look lovely, Mum. I'm very proud of you," he said with genuine warmth. She'd trimmed down considerably over the past month and with her hair restyled, she looked ten years younger.

She flushed with pleasure, though his compliment didn't quite erase the touch of anxiety in her eyes. "I just hope you'll be happy, Matt," she said softly, caringly.

He nodded, momentarily too choked up to speak. He loved his mother. He wanted her to be happy for him. It was probably the idea of him suddenly belonging to someone else that had upset her. Once the marriage was fact...

The raised sound of commotion outside the church distracted both of them. "The cars must have arrived," his mother murmured.

Matt checked his watch. Eleven o'clock, on the dot. Relief poured into a quickly rising sense of elation. Everything was fine. Peta wanted this marriage as much as he did. She was right on time.

The guests who had waited outside for the arrival of the bridal party started trickling into the church. First amongst them was Father O'Malley who'd been greeting those he knew at the church door. An old family friend, he'd married Peta's parents and had officiated at all the Kelly christenings and marriages since then. Peta had insisted on having him conduct their wedding ceremony, though he was now in a retirement home and, in Matt's private opinion, a bit on the vague and doddery side.

He beamed benevolently at Matt, and fussily ushered him and Tony to their positions in front of the altar, ready for the entrance of the bride. "Big day, big day...got to get it right," he babbled to himself, the excitement of the occasion causing him considerable nervous agitation.

The strain on Matt's nerves had eased. He felt quite calm, watching the guests settle themselves in the pews, nodding and smiling at friends, his secretary, other highly valued employees. Peta's mother, accompanied by her eldest son, Paul, was the last to take her place. There was a happy hum of anticipation in the church. It started to tingle through Matt as the music began.

His gaze flipped over the two flower girls leading the procession down the aisle—Paul's daughters, decked out in cream and gold like little princesses. It fastened on Megan, Peta's sister and matron of honour, a pretty blonde who had a subtle way of getting what she wanted. Peta's bold spontaneity obviously pained her.

She'd pasted a smile on her face that glittered as brightly as her golden dress, yet to Matt, it had a false brightness. He'd sensed a reserve in Megan from their very first meeting and it hadn't gone away. Whatever her reasons, she was no more in favour of this marriage than his mother was.

But it didn't matter anymore.

Peta was here.

As Megan stepped up from the aisle, leaving his view of Peta and her father unimpeded, Matt's breath caught in his throat. *His bride...* It was a moment of utter enchantment. She looked like some magical, medieval queen moving regally towards him; her highnecked, long-sleeved gown sheening her curves with deep cream satin, moulding her fantastic figure to her hipline where a band of pearls and gold braid held a skirt that fell in graceful folds, gradually flowing out into a long train. A similar pearl and gold band encircled her hair, supporting a veil that floated around her face, giving it an air of seductive mystery.

His heart seemed to swell. Her stunning femininity called to everything male in him. He wanted to lay the world at her feet. He wanted to hold her safe from all hurt. Like the knights of old he'd do battle for this woman. She was a queen...*his* queen.

Her father released her and she stepped up to stand beside him, offering her hand. It was trembling. Matt suddenly felt the gravity of what they were doing—pledging themselves to each other, entering an intimate togetherness that would span the rest of their lives. All that had gone before was ending now with the vows they were about to exchange, and he was acutely conscious of the responsibilities he was undertaking as he took his bride's hand in his.

Through the filmy veil misting the vivid beauty of her face, he saw the deep blue sea of vulnerability in her eyes, and silently, fervently promised her it would be all right. He would take every care of her. Her lips moved into a quivery smile and he sensed her trying to hold fear at bay, to bravely commit herself to him, and Matt was so caught up in transmitting reassurance, he barely followed the words of the ceremony.

There was some kind of general address about marriage from Father O'Malley, readings from the Bible that he knew Peta had selected as meaningful to her—lead-ups to the serious business of sealing their promises to each other. Then the moment was upon him and he repeated each phrase intoned by Father O'Malley, his pulse thumping so hard it seemed to roar in his ears.

"I, Matthew Jeremy Davis…take you, Peta Mary Kelly…"

He completed his part and to his utter bewilderment, the gravity of Peta's expression started to disintegrate, first with a twitching smile which she couldn't suppress, then her eyes dancing with unholy amusement, finally a giggle which was so inappropriate it sparked panic in Matt. Was she struck with some form of hysteria? Did it mean she was about to back out?

He had the ring in his hand, ready to slide it onto her finger but she was holding her palm up to stop him. The effort to control herself was obvious. A few titters ran around the congregation. Nervous reaction to imminent disaster, Matt wildly reasoned. He himself was paralysed by it.

The priest hadn't noticed anything amiss. Peta leaned over and grasped his arm, halting him in the midst of, "I, Peta Mary..."

Halting him before he came to declaring them husband and wife!

Matt's heart dropped like a stone.

"Father, I think you'd better do Matt's vow again," she gently advised him. "It got a bit muddled. You just guided him into promising to be my wife."

"Oh!" Father O'Malley looked mortified. "Oh, my goodness! I do beg your pardon, Matthew. My eyes must have skipped to the next vow. They're not as sharp as they used to be. I was thinking Peta will make a wonderful wife...good stock, you know, the Kellys..."

Relief burst into a grin that almost rioted into a peal of laughter as Matt's whole body churned from despair to a bubbling sense of the ridiculous. "It's okay, Father," he had to choke out. "Let's rerun it."

Peta was biting her lips through the whole repetition. Her shoulders were shaking. She kept her eyes downcast and Matt knew she was brimming with laughter. It was all he could do to keep serious himself. This time, however, her hand was spread ready to receive the wedding ring and Matt felt a huge well of satisfaction as he slid it home.

Then it was Peta's turn. She took a deep breath, stared fixedly at his mouth, spoke each phrase with a tremulousness that bordered on breaking down, then lifted her gaze with a look of twinkling triumph as she enunced the last words... ''...Your lawful wedded wife.''

They grinned at each other, a mad zany grin that wiped out all the nervousness of doubts and fears. Laughter broke all barriers, Matt thought exultantly, and as they were finally declared husband and wife, he felt a bonding that went far deeper than words, a sense of sharing that would take them through every trial and tribulation. They could always laugh together.

''You may kiss the bride.''

Matt lifted Peta's veil. He knew it was supposed to be a dignified kiss. A cavalier sense of mischief seized him. He bent Peta over his arm in exuberant tango style, ravished her astonished mouth, and before she could catch her breath, scooped her off her feet and weighed her in his arms like a pirate appraising his booty.

''Matt! Put me down,'' she insisted.

''My wedding ring is on your finger,'' he reminded her, whispering in her ear. ''The vestry is only ten paces to my right.''

''What?'' She looked befuddled.

The congregation was clapping.

''We can get back to our appreciative guests much faster if you're not wearing pants.''

She focused on his teasing eyes and began to laugh. ''You can't...get past...my chastity belt,'' she gasped out between giggles.

''What?''

"No key…until you've signed…the marriage certificate."

"Okay."

He carried her over to the table set for the final deed and sat her down on the chair which Tony, grinning from ear to ear, had swiftly drawn out for her. Even Megan had a genuine smile on her face as they went through the last formalities of signing and witnessing the marriage certificate. Matt felt so happy he was right in tune with the song being sung, "I Finally Found Someone."

Not even the taking of an excessive amount of photographs dimmed his good humour. Then it was party time at the reception place Peta had chosen and the next few hours flashed by him, which seemed odd, because most wedding receptions he'd been to tended to drag on. Somehow it was different with his own.

Occasionally there were awkward moments when some of the guests—mostly Peta's aunts—gushed over him with sentiments he wasn't quite comfortable with. Women did get very mushy at weddings. However, he was delighted to see his mother getting on well with the Kelly clan. They were nice people. He looked forward to being part of their family.

They were certainly a productive lot. Paul had four children, two boys, two girls. John had three, all boys, his wife pregnant with the fourth, hoping for a girl this time. Megan only had the one so far but she was the youngest. Matt understood Peta feeling like a very late starter in the family stakes, understood about the tests, too.

Just as well he'd passed the sperm count with flying colours. Though, of course, he'd had every confidence he would. Nothing amiss with Peta's fertility, either. Not that he'd imagined there would be. A woman built like Peta was made to have babies. This time next year...

The urge to check out if Peta *was* wearing pants was very strong.

Wrong time and place, he sternly told himself. He needed hours to do all he wanted to do with her. A rushed coupling in a broom cupboard would not suffice, however tempting and exciting the thought was. Besides, the long train on her dress probably wouldn't fit into a broom cupboard. Maybe the cloakroom... No, he'd waited this long. Tonight would come fast enough. Their first time together should have some class to it. But he sure was ready for it!

His mother grabbed him as he was circulating amongst his friends, Peta having been snaffled from his side by her nieces who were demanding yet another photo opportunity.

"Do you know Peta's mother is only the same age as me?" she said in wonderment.

"You look younger, Mum," he declared. "You look great. I bet all the older guys here have been flirting with you." It felt as though champagne was fizzing through his blood, though he'd barely drunk a glass of it.

She laughed and shook her head. "You *are* a wicked boy today! I was just amazed she already has eight grandchildren and another on the way."

"Well, I'll be working on it for you, Mum. I'll throw my whole heart into it. Not to mention my body. Four grandchildren coming up."

"You didn't really marry Peta for me, though, did you?" she pressed.

"Nope. All for me, Mum. Look at her! She's my queen."

"Your father used to call me that." She heaved a deep sigh. "I do hope Peta lives up to it for you, dear."

"No worries on that score," he said with ringing confidence.

"Her mother was just telling me how pleased all the family is that you rescued her from some terrible affair with an Italian." She paused, looked hesitant, then scanned his eyes anxiously. "She's not still hankering after him, is she, Matt?"

"As far as Peta is concerned, the guy is buried, Mum. The future is ours," he assured her.

At that moment, Matt felt absolutely secure in that belief.

The Bridal Waltz was announced and he moved to claim Peta from her family. She was laughing up at him as he whirled her onto the small dance floor with all the panache of Fred Astaire. Matt was revelling in *panache* today. He loved the sparkle it put in Peta's beautiful blue eyes.

"Ladies and gentlemen," the master of ceremonies called pompously, "I give you Mr. and Mrs. Matt Davis."

Unaccountably the sparkle was suddenly drowned

by a welling of tears. Matt swept Peta into a close embrace as he led her into the waltz. "Something wrong?" he murmured anxiously.

"No…" She burrowed closer, hiding her face. "A bit emotional…that's all."

Weddings, Matt thought. Women always shed tears at weddings. Nothing to worry about. He felt a rush of tenderness. It was probably nervous exhaustion with Peta. He'd take it slowly tonight, make her feel really good about everything, especially having him as her husband. He'd be a lot better for her than the Latin lover.

Matt frowned over that last thought. He didn't want to get into comparisons. He hoped Peta wouldn't, either. Their relationship was different. It meant more. It had to mean more. He was going to be the father of her children.

The rest of the bridal party joined them on the dance floor, his mother waltzing with one of Peta's uncles. Partners were exchanged and Matt reluctantly passed Peta to her father. She was blinking furiously and clutched her dad as though he was a raft in stormy seas.

He found himself dancing with Megan and tried to steer a steady course through his troubled mind. "You did a fine job helping Peta today, Megan," he said, giving her due credit.

"You're a good guy, Matt," she answered with a hint of strain. "I'm glad she found you."

The words were generous. Perhaps he was oversensitive right now. He heard a "but…" in them and couldn't stop himself from trying to nail it. "But...?" he prompted, looking directly into her eyes.

They were blue, too, but not as vivid a blue as Peta's. He saw the flash of uncertainty in them, then the deep concern emerging. "You *will* hold on to her, won't you, Matt? No matter what?"

Why wouldn't he? Matt frowned at her, disliking the doubt she'd raised. "I never make promises I don't intend to keep, Megan," he asserted strongly.

She shook her head. "I didn't mean..." A sigh, an apologetic grimace, a look of appeal. "Forgive me. This has happened so fast... I truly do wish you and Peta every happiness."

What had she meant?

No use pursuing it. She'd closed off. Matt tried to make sense of what she'd said. If her doubts weren't centred on him...what did she know about Peta that he didn't?

The thought unsettled him further. He hated the feeling, needed to get rid of it. His instincts raged for positive action. He danced Megan straight over to her father and reclaimed Peta, almost crushing her to him in needful fervour. She was his. He wanted her...every part of her. The yearning ripped through his body, barely containable.

She wound her arms around his neck, her over-bright eyes questioning his, her cheeks flushing as though suffused with the blast of heat coming from him.

"I'm dying for you," he said bluntly.

"I want you, too, Matt," she answered, fueling a

desire that rocketed to intense urgency. "There's a change room waiting for us. We could go there now."

Change room? He'd forgotten that one. "Peta…" He struggled with his previous intention to wait for less limited time.

"I need you right now," she said, her eyes flaring with the irresistible promise of instant satisfaction, hot, hard and reckless. "Come with me."

Come with her! Wild horses couldn't stop him.

She took his hand and led him off the dance floor. "Going to change, Mum," she said as they passed her parents who were now dancing together.

"Do you want help, dear?"

"I've got my husband to help me."

My husband. It sounded good to Matt. It sounded great!

No holding back from Peta.

She had his wedding ring on her finger—the symbol of good faith—and she wanted him in her pants every bit as much as he wanted to be there.

No matter what!

It was more than enough to zoom Matt's confidence in their future together sky-high.

CHAPTER ELEVEN

"BETTER lock the door, Matt."

The provocative lilt of her voice and the hot simmer in her eyes had Matt spinning to do her bidding. There was no key. No keyhole. His mind blanked in frustration for a moment, then snapped into high gear. Button on the doorknob. He clicked in the lock.

Peta had already unfastened her veil and tossed it on the chaise longue. He did a double take. Chaise longue? Ridiculous piece of furniture! There was only that and a couple of fancy antique chairs. Clothes rack by the window. Peta moving to stand in front of a cheval mirror. Nothing so handy as a bed in sight!

"Undo me?"

Peta slid a suggestive look at him over her shoulder. Matt instantly forgot about a bed. She had her back turned to him, one hand indicating the buttons at the back of her high collar, the other sweeping the train out of his way. He sprang into action, the erotic pleasure of *undoing* increasingly stimulating as he released buttons, found the head of the zipper and opened up the whole length of her bodice, baring a creamy expanse of skin and an extremely sexy corselet concocted of satin ribbons and lace.

Peta whipped her arms out of her long sleeves while Matt was still examining the exotic piece of lingerie, wondering how it undid. Then the dress dropped and he was staring at bare buttocks; beautifully rounded, firm, naked flesh, interrupted only by lacy suspenders attached to silk stockings.

"You're not wearing pants!" The words shot off his tongue in sheer shock.

"Disappointed?"

"Hell, no!"

His gaze flew up to assure her he was mightily impressed. She was watching him in the mirror, a bold challenge in her eyes. The realisation thumped through him that ever since she'd walked down the aisle to him she'd been like this under her wedding dress, earlier than that, getting ready for him, making herself easily accessible so that once they were married, she really *was* his whenever he wanted. And she had to be wanting, too, conscious of her waiting nakedness all these hours....

Matt was too stunned to move. His gaze was drawn to the full reflection of her in the mirror, his mind dazzled by the seductive display of her sexuality. Her beautiful breasts swelled opulently above scalloped cups of peek-through lace, deliberately designed to be transparent over the darker area of her aureoles so her nipples stood out invitingly.

The ribbons on the corselet angled in to emphasise the smallness of her waist, then fanned out to highlight the lush curve of her hips. Lacy suspenders framed the bare apex of her thighs where an arrowhead of tightly curled hair waited for his touch, waited to be parted and spread for him, and he was so rock-hard and ready, *his* pants could barely hold him.

He dragged his gaze up to hers. "I could not imagine a more desirable woman," he said, his voice so low and furry he barely recognised it.

Primitive instincts were running riot, the male animal in him stirred to fever-pitch, yet he wanted to prolong this moment of revelation, savouring the incredible sexiness of her and the deliberately blatant gift of it to him. An old saying floated through his mind... *Start as you mean to go on.* If this was Peta's intent, he had himself a marriage made in heaven!

"I've tried to imagine you, Matt. Will you show me? All of you?"

The husky appeal drove him wild. He'd been fantasising about her for weeks, day and night, and the reality was blowing his mind, but the thought of her fantasising about him was even more explosive. He hurled off his jacket. He almost strangled himself getting his bow tie undone. The studs on his shirt went flying. Shoes, socks...

She swung around to watch him, sliding off her high-heeled shoes, leaving her lovely, long, silk-clad legs slightly apart. Her gaze seemed to gloat over the taut muscles of his shoulders and arms. As he straightened up to unfasten his trousers, her focus moved to the hair on his chest, the dark line of it that ran down to his navel. He was acutely, excruciatingly aware of his fiercely aroused state. At last he was released from all constriction, his pants kicked away, and he stood with his manhood on uninhibited display, his heart pumping blood through him at a chaotic rate.

She stared at him, her breathing quick and shallow. She touched herself, her fingers sliding to her cleft as though wondering how he would feel there, and it was beyond Matt's capacity to remain apart from her any longer. In sheer blind lust he moved and she met him, sheathing his erection with her hand as she pulled him with her onto the floor, urging their coupling in a frenzy of movement, uncaring of the clothes strewn underneath them, wanting him, demanding him, pushing, thrusting, arching.

Impossible not to follow her insistent direction. Impossible not to plunge straight into her, tunneling fiercely, heat enveloping him, her silky flesh pulsing around him, her thighs gripping his hips, legs locked around his buttocks, driving him deep, a savage cry from her throat stirring the beast in him, throwing him completely out of control.

Her breasts spilled out of their lace cups, lushly inviting. He couldn't stop to touch them. Her mouth lay open, gasping, emitting sexy sounds of satisfaction, her lips pouting sensually. He couldn't stop to kiss them. The need to keep pounding into her erased every other fantasy he'd entertained.

This deep inner world she gave him craved all he could give. He felt it in every cell of his body—the mating call—and he responded to it mindlessly, helplessly in thrall to the rhythm of it, loving the wildness of it, exulting in the roll of climactic spasms he felt coming from her. Her thighs were quivering, yet still she held him to her, willing him to take her further.

He exerted himself even more, changing the direction of thrust and contact, making her feel him everywhere, and the throb of her around him excited him beyond bearing. Every muscle in his body screamed for release. He couldn't hold it any longer. As though she sensed him on the edge, she lifted herself, and he spilled himself into her, a last vital pumping that left him drained, yet so sweetly replete.

Her sigh feathered his face as he slumped forward and Matt knew instinctively it was a sigh of completion. He was too dazed to think. He gathered her to him and rested content, breathing in her scent, basking in her soft warmth, at peace with the marriage they had just consummated.

Peta smiled to herself as she floated back to earth again, deeply gratified that this first mating had been fast and furious and fulfilling the need to forget for a while what she had done today. She would be fine now. She could carry it off...being the wife Matt wanted. There was no reason to feel guilty about not loving him. Great sex covered a lot of shortcomings and they could certainly have that.

Her newly wedded husband was incredibly well endowed. Not even Giorgio, who'd been quite vain about his manhood...she winced at the insidious comparison, pushing it out of her mind. She had to overlay her memory of him with the life she'd have with Matt. It was starting now. No more tears for a lost love. No more nervous apprehensions. No more wondering and worrying.

She might be conceiving a baby right at this minute. And wouldn't that be marvellous! Maybe a boy…if he inherited his father's physique he'd be perfect. Peta doubted there could be a more beautiful male body than Matt's.

The strength and power of him…her inner muscles spasmed again with the pleasure of having felt so much. He could drive her mindless with the sheer explosion of physical sensation and that was good. It concentrated her whole being on him, on the togetherness they could forge. And they would. She would make it happen…the kind of family unit she wanted…her husband, her children.

A fierce wave of possessiveness swept through her. She'd taken this man at his word and his word had proved good. *He* was good. In every way. She wished she could feel more for him but at least he was hers, every bit of him hers, and she would keep it that way, giving him as much of herself as she could. He'd been fair with her. No cheating. She'd return that fairness in full measure.

"Matt…" She ran her fingernails down his back.

He lifted his head, his clear grey eyes mirroring intense sexual satisfaction.

She smiled, lifting her hand to stroke his cheek. "I'm not disappointed, either."

His mouth stretched into a wide lecherous grin. "You, my darling wife, are a tiger. And let me give you an open invitation to eat me any time you like."

"Thank you." Her eyes flirted teasingly with his. "I love the way you fill me up."

He laughed, heaving himself off her. "Guess we should be making a move." His eyes sparkled with happy anticipation. "Tonight, I'm going to eat you, Peta Davis."

"Ah...a consuming passion." She squirmed provocatively. "I'll look forward to it."

He hauled her up and caught her against him, his hands sliding down to cup her bottom, gently squeezing her soft flesh. "Thank you for this," he said gruffly.

"A mutual pleasure," she answered, winding her arms around his neck.

She kissed him. He kissed her. It was like champagne after strawberries and cream, and Peta wallowed in the sweet intoxication of it, wanting to lose herself in him. It worked until it ended.

Then it was necessary to deal with practical realities. It was lucky there was an ensuite bathroom where they could wash and tidy up. They had to get dressed and face their guests again, take their leave of them.

Peta assured herself she could do it with confidence now. She would respond happily to her parents' good wishes and her brothers' good-humoured teasing, and she would look Megan straight in the eye and defy her sister's doubts. She'd chosen right. She was going to enjoy every minute of her honeymoon.

They cleared up the change room, then looked at each other with a delicious sense of guilty pleasure.

"Ready?" Matt asked, his eyes simmering over the slinky knit suit she had donned.

She returned the sexy appraisal, proud to be this man's wife. Even in his dark grey suit, Matt would turn any woman's head. "Where are you going to start?" she asked.

"What?" His gaze clung to her breasts.

"Eating me."

He laughed, his eyes dancing with pleasure. "Why do you want to know?"

"So I can think about it."

"Toes," he said. "Definitely toes. While I think about what else is waiting for me."

Her stomach flipped over and her toes started curling. "Okay, I'm ready," she declared. With orgasmic toes on her mind, goodbyes would be a breeze.

Matt took her hand and together they went back to the reception room to complete their last wedding duties.

They were married.

Next step...children.

And making them would be no hardship.

CHAPTER TWELVE

THE last night of their honeymoon…

The best two weeks of his life, Matt thought. No question. Far North Queensland was the perfect escape from the cold winter in Sydney and The Mirage Resort at Port Douglas had been an inspired choice, given that Peta hadn't wanted to travel outside Australia. Golf, tennis, swimming, snorkelling off the Great Barrier Reef, whitewater rafting through tropical rainforest…they'd done it all, each beautiful sunny day lived to the full, and the nights…ah, the nights…

He sat back with his glass of wine and watched Peta pick through the last of the coral trout on her plate. They'd chosen to come into town and dine at Portofino's, a fine Italian restaurant in the main street, a more casual, intimate setting than the hotel provided. Their table was in a corner of its courtyard, shadowed by the heavily foliaged branches of a mango tree. It was a soft balmy evening and Peta had worn an orange sundress. She glowed in the candlelight.

Matt could hardly believe his luck in having met her—met her and married her. She was everything he'd ever wanted in a woman; fun company, great to play with, enjoying the challenge and the thrill of all the activities they'd shared, very much a matching partner…especially in bed. He'd never had such great sex. Nor so often. He only had to look at her—think of her—to be turned on and she was wickedly, wonderfully uninhibited about encouraging him, not to mention pleasuring him as thoroughly as he hoped he pleasured her.

Her lightly tanned skin gleamed like satin. He had to restrain himself from reaching out to run his fingertips over it. The bodice of her dress was moulded to her figure, the neckline low enough to reveal a tantalising cleavage. He knew she wasn't wearing a bra and he started to get hard, remembering how she'd drawn him into that soft valley and pushed her breasts together, laughingly telling him he was trapped in a landslide.

Matt sipped the cold white wine and forced himself to relax. The night was young. Peta had said she fancied a dessert after her fish—something sweet and sinfully full of calories. Racing her off before her appetite was satisfied would be selfish. He wanted her to have everything she wanted, especially this last night.

"Enjoy it?" he asked as she sat back from her meal with a satisfied sigh.

"Truly superb. Perfectly cooked. Was your fettuccine good?"

"Fine."

As he took the bottle of wine out of the cooler and leaned across to refill her glass, he spotted a woman with a flower basket offering single red roses, trying to interest the male diners into buying one for their ladies. The romantic gesture appealed to Matt, something a little special on the last night of their honeymoon. Having topped up Peta's wine, he replaced the bottle and signalled the woman over, taking out his wallet in readiness.

"How much?" he asked, not caring what it cost.

"Five dollars, sir," came the smiling answer.

"No, Matt..." Peta jack-knifed forward to halt the purchase, grabbing his arm, waving an agitated dismissal to the seller, her eyes sharp with rejection. "Please don't!"

"Why not?" Her protest made no sense to him.

She looked at a loss for a moment, then seized on a reason. "It would be a waste. We're leaving in the morning."

"It's only one rose," he argued. "I want you to have it."

"No. It's silly," she insisted.

"Oh, I don't know." He handed the woman a five dollar note and took the rose, smiling at Peta as he leaned forward and trailed the soft petals down her bare arm. "I can think of some uses for it."

She recoiled, as though her skin crawled from the caress. Her eyes flared with hot hatred.

Matt froze, stunned by her reaction.

She huddled back in her chair, hugging her arms, clearly stressed, her gaze flicking away from his, lashes lowering to hide her expression.

Very slowly he laid the offending rose on the table and eased back in his chair, feeling her tension like a knife in his gut. He didn't understand what he'd done wrong. A bit of playful sensuality should have been harmless fun. They'd toyed with teasing suggestiveness many times, enjoying it.

"Peta?" he called softly, hating the sense of separation that had sliced between them.

She rubbed her arms as though she was suddenly cold. The temperature of the night hadn't changed. The difference came from inside her...mental, emotional, physical? Matt was totally bewildered by it, and she wasn't answering, her eyes still downcast, her face closed to him.

"I'm sorry," he said quietly. "I didn't mean to upset you."

"I told you I didn't want it," she excused herself in a tight little voice.

Their waitress arrived to collect their plates. Seeing a way out of the contretemps, Matt quickly picked up the rose and handed it to her. "Take this, too," he commanded.

It surprised her. "For me?"

"Yes."

She smiled. "Thank you."

The natural response, making Peta's seem even more unnatural. The waitress gave her a questioning look which wasn't met and promptly left them to a cleared table, scooting away from any argument.

"It's gone," he stated matter-of-factly, trying to lower the wall Peta had wrapped around herself.

She dragged in a deep breath and released it in a long, shuddering sigh. He could see the effort it cost her to lift her gaze to his and there was pain in her eyes. "I don't want you to ever give me roses, Matt."

"May I ask why not?"

She winced and looked down again. "They're used...wrongly. They bring back bad memories. I don't want to feel that way. Not with you."

The Latin lover! Her description of that affair sliced into Matt's mind...*surprises, romantic settings, lovely gifts.* He'd probably showered her with flowers, maybe even using them in making love to her. Two years of it, leading to nothing but bitter disillusionment! And she was still *bleeding* from him!

The knife in Matt's gut twisted. Was all they'd shared since their wedding a pretence on her side? Didn't it mean anything to her? Why did she have to bring *him* into it?

Anger spurted over the angst she'd stirred. Where was the clean slate he'd offered her? Just because that cheating bastard had given her roses, did that mean he couldn't, not even out of genuine feeling for her? Couldn't she see the difference? She wore his wedding ring, for God's sake!

He could feel his face tightening, his whole body screwing up at the violation to his feelings for her. "I don't care to have roses banned from *our life,* Peta," he bit out, barely able to hold back a jealous tirade.

It galvanised her attention. She stared at him for several long tension-ridden moments. Finally she said, "Red roses are supposed to symbolise love, Matt." As though suddenly conscious of her guarded posture, she unfolded her arms and rested her hands on the table, palms open in a gesture of appeal as she wryly added, "That's not what we have, is it?"

He stared back at her, jolted into a painful realisation that her view of their relationship did not encompass any sense of him being someone uniquely special for her. "What do we have, Peta?" he asked quietly, feeling he was treading the edge of a precipice and there was a deep black chasm right in front of him.

Her mouth moved into an ironic little smile. "You said it yourself...a marriage of convenience...for the sake of having a family."

The reasoning he'd used to get her...handed straight back to him. Never mind that it was eight weeks on. For her, nothing had changed. Nothing at all. While for him... He struggled to put it in perspective. Quite simply...the world had moved.

Matt hauled himself away from the chasm created by the rage of his own feelings. As much as he now recoiled from the logical reality of what he had proposed to Peta, it was safe ground, he fiercely told himself, a stable platform from which he could work forward.

She was his wife. He'd won that much. She'd just made it plain—once more—that she didn't love him, and he could hardly blame her for her honesty. It hurt. It hurt more than he'd ever imagined it could. He could barely contain it. Yet he had to. It wouldn't be fair to take his disappointment out on Peta, simply because he'd expected more than she was ready to

give. He'd assumed too much, colouring her feelings
with his own.

Time...

Matt clung to *time* as the answer to his need.

Forget the Latin lover.

Jealousy would only erode the togetherness that
was possible between them. It wasn't an easy thing
to discard emotional baggage, even though it didn't
relate to anything he'd done to her. He had to be patient, give her time for it to fade into the background,
keep her mind occupied with all that was good in their
marriage.

Her hands moved to lie flat on the table. She
stroked a finger over the rings he'd given her. Her
face was grave, sad. It squeezed his heart.

"I'm sorry, Matt." She lifted regretful eyes. "I've
spoilt tonight, haven't I?"

He cursed the impulse that had shattered his illu-
sions. Yet wasn't it better for his blinkers to be ripped
off before he made other foolish assumptions? Accept
what you have and do your best with it, he silently
commanded.

The will to recover what had been lost prompted a
shrug and a smile. "My mistake." He couldn't stop
himself from adding hopefully, "All we've shared
this past fortnight...it just didn't feel like a convenience to me."

He waved dismissively, not wanting it to sound like
an accusation, putting her under pressure to reply.

She relaxed back in her chair and he saw her gather
the determination to move past this fracture. She

wanted to mend it. The wish—the need—was in her eyes as she tried a teasing smile. "Mutual lust can go a long way."

Matt snatched up the ball and ran with it. "And highly pleasurable it is, too." He managed an appreciative grin.

"It's been a wonderful honeymoon, Matt," she pressed on with a rush of warmth. "We've had so much fun."

"I've enjoyed every minute of it," he rolled out with relish.

"Me, too. Especially the whitewater rafting. Though it was so scary at one point my heart was in my mouth."

Matt effected a quizzical look. "Have I pushed you further than you wanted to go?"

She laughed and shook her head.

They bantered on, recalling the high moments they'd shared, doing their utmost to recapture the mood of taking pleasure in each other, pushing the bad stuff behind them.

But for Matt, it didn't go away, no matter how hard he worked at it. He sensed it didn't go away for Peta, either. They covered it up but it lay underneath everything they said and did, a dark area overlaid with bubble and froth.

Peta forced herself to eat the cheesecake she'd ended up ordering because they were pretending so hard that everything was all right.

But it wasn't all right.

She'd hurt him.

Hurt him because of what Giorgio had done to her, because she'd believed in Giorgio's roses...and she was a fool. Matt was innocent of any falseness. He'd given her the substance of marriage, committed himself fully to making it work and she'd slapped him down for wanting to give a token of his pleasure in her.

It was mean...it was wrong...though however mean and wrong it was, she could not have borne Matt using the rose as a sensual aid in their intimacy. Impossible to forget that Giorgio had done precisely the same thing. She didn't want the memory of *him* in bed with her and Matt. She didn't want the memory of *him* anywhere in her marriage.

Yet she'd just put it there with her revulsion to the caress of the rose. And the explanation she'd felt compelled to give.

The whole incident had happened so fast, it had caught her unprepared, reacting instead of realising the effect of such a reaction on Matt. Now the damage was done and couldn't be undone. She could see it in his eyes, despite the cheerful facade he'd done his best to adopt.

She'd hurt him.

She'd hurt their relationship which she'd come to value very highly these past two weeks. What they had together was good, much better than... *cheesecake!*

Giorgio had thrown sweets at her for two years.

The cheesecake sickened her.

The guilt and shame churning through her stomach

would not accept any more *sweets*. She wanted what Matt gave her…the solid bread and butter of friendship, caring, consideration of her needs and wants, and she wanted to give the same back to him.

She put down the spoon.

"Not to your liking?" Matt asked.

She met his inquiring gaze squarely. "I'd rather have you."

His carefully constructed composure cracked and desire leapt out at her.

Peta's heart lifted. "Let's get out of here, Matt, and go back to the hotel."

"I won't argue with that," he said with a fervour that told her he shared the need to wipe out any third person from their marriage.

Peta vowed she would make him forget everything but the two of them…together. It was the last night of their honeymoon. It belonged to them.

CHAPTER THIRTEEN

"IT'S your wife, Matt," his secretary informed, aware he'd been hanging on this call for the past hour, his concentration on work shot to pieces this morning.

He snatched up the telephone. "Peta?" His voice had climbed with anticipation and he cursed himself for it. If she was disappointed...

"I'm pregnant!"

"The blood test was positive?"

"Absolutely. No doubt about it."

Relief spurted into joy. "That's great, Peta! Great!"

"We're going to have a baby, Matt."

The happiness in her voice bubbled through him like a champagne cocktail. "It's wonderful news! The best!" Elation topped it off. They'd done it! First hit! Only five weeks since their wedding day and Peta was positively pregnant. "How do you feel?" he asked, grinning from ear to ear.

"So excited I could burst. I can't wait to tell everyone."

"Where are you now?"

"Still at the doctor's office."

Matt wished he was with her but she'd insisted he go to work, saying it was silly to take time off when her missed period might only be a hiccup in her nor-

mal cycle. Matt suspected she'd been protecting herself against *his* disappointment. They'd both been riding high on hope this past week.

"I'm going home now to spread the good news,"
she crowed triumphantly. "I'll let you tell your
mother, Matt."

He laughed. No doubt she'd be on the telephone
for hours. "I'll come home early. This calls for a
celebration. We'll go out for dinner."

"No. Let's eat in. I'll buy something special and
we'll have an intimate dinner for three. You, me and
our first child."

Her sigh brimmed with heartfelt satisfaction. Matt
felt a tightness in his chest himself. "A family celebration," he said huskily. "I'll bring the very best
champagne."

"That would be lovely," she enthused. "'Bye for
now."

Gone before he could hold her talking to him
longer. Some of the fizz died with the disconnection
but Matt assured himself it would return in full measure this evening. A happy celebration. The happiest.
A baby gave them a very solid footing for their marriage to go forward.

Not that it wasn't highly satisfactory already. No
man in his right mind could knock mutual lust and
there'd been plenty of it since the night of the rose
incident. For a brief niggling moment, he wondered
if Peta's desire for him would ease off now she had
what she most wanted. Was he just a stud to her?

He shook off the thought. Stupid to spoil the pleasure of this day. Besides, their relationship was just as good out of bed as in it. He couldn't ask for a more companionable partner. Nothing was going to affect that. With a baby on the way, they'd have even more to talk about and plan for.

Smiling, he dialled his mother's telephone number. She answered on the second ring. "Cynthia Davis," she rattled off as though in a hurry.

"It's Matt."

"Hello, dear! I'm just off to the Bridge Club. Can we chat this evening instead?"

Bridge Club, View Club, an Asian cooking course—Thai, Chinese, Vietnamese—weekly Tai Chi sessions…his mother had certainly thrown herself into activities these past few months, making good her promise to establish a new life for herself. Matt was delighted at the efforts she had made to pick up and pursue interests.

"No, I'll be busy this evening," he answered. "I thought you'd like to know Peta's pregnant with your first grandchild."

"What? Already!" she gasped.

"You could say, 'Congratulations,'" Matt teased.

"Of course. Congratulations, dear. To both of you," she gushed. "Though it is early days, Matt. I do hope…well, you are old enough to know what you're doing."

He grimaced…still the doubt about his rushing into marriage with Peta. And now parenthood. "It *is* what we want, Mum," he assured her.

"Oh, it's lovely news, dear. My first grandchild.

Wouldn't it be wonderful if it was a girl? I'd be able to buy all the things I couldn't buy for a boy. What a thrill!''

He laughed. "I can't guarantee a girl.''

"No.'' She laughed at herself. "Don't mind me. It doesn't really matter as long as the baby's healthy. I'll love it anyway. My first grandchild.''

It was good to hear the pride and pleasure in her voice.

"Have you thought of any names yet?'' she asked hopefully.

"No. Maybe we'll do that tonight.''

"Well, tell Peta I'll call her tomorrow since you're busy tonight. Lots of love to both of you, dear.''

"Thanks, Mum. Have a good bridge game.''

She sighed. "I won't be able to concentrate now. Never mind. I'll have happy thoughts.''

On that uplifting note, Matt was happy to end the call. He walked over to the door leading into his secretary's office, opened it and stood there, smiling benevolently at the woman who had advised taking his mother to the health farm.

Rita Sutcliffe was in her early fifties, a widow who'd been out of the work force for years before Matt took her on as his secretary, mostly because she could actually spell, partly because she'd brought up five children which proved considerable organisational skills, as well as having a wealth of common sense which appealed to him.

Her health farm idea had been a stroke of genius. So much good had eventuated from it, both for himself and his mother, he'd be forever grateful to Rita. Apart from which, she was a thoroughly nice person who always had his best interests at heart, both personally and professionally.

"Would you like a week at the health farm, Rita?"

"What?"

"Make your choice. It's either that or a nine month's free supply of Belgian chocolates."

"What?" she repeated, unable to make sense of this sudden rush of beneficence.

"Well, I can't give out cigars. I've given up smoking and it's not politically correct."

He could see her mind go clickety-click as she added it up and grinned sheer delight at him. "A baby."

"Fatherhood, here I come!"

"Good for you! And Peta! I'm so pleased for you." She laughed. "And for me! I'll take a raincheck on the week at the health farm. I'll need it after the chocolate deluge at Christmas."

"Fine! Mark it into the calendar and I'll foot the bill."

'What about flowers?"

"You want flowers, too?"

She rolled her eyes at him. "For the mother-to-be. I think at least a dozen red roses is in order. Shall I call a florist for you?"

"No. Not roses."

He frowned, not liking the reminder of Peta's restriction. That cheating bastard in Rome would never have given her a child. Nevertheless, Matt didn't want even a whiff of a memory of him around Peta on this special day. Roses were out. Yet the idea of flowers appealed so strongly he was reluctant to discard it. Why shouldn't he send them? She was his wife. She was carrying his baby.

"Can I get blue flowers at this time of year?" he asked. Rita always knew that kind of stuff.

"Irises. Though you can't count on having a boy, Matt," she added wisely.

"What's pink?"

"Carnations, tulips…"

"Tulips," he decided. They were more unusual than carnations and without any romantic connotations. "Blue irises and pink tulips. Get a bunch of each delivered, Rita, and have them put on the card— *To celebrate our boy or girl!*"

"Signed… Love, Matt?" Rita queried, writing the message down.

It was on the tip of his tongue to say, "Yes." Then realising Peta might think it glib—though it wasn't— he hunted for other words, trying not to sound any false note with her.

"No," he said slowly. "I think… *From Daddy.*"

Rita laughed. "One besotted father coming up."

It restored Matt's good humour. Peta would readily accept a gift on behalf of their child and derive pleasure from it. He was on safe ground there. As long as he held on, chances were he'd win everything in the end.

*   *   *

"When are you planning on giving up your job?" Megan asked.

"I haven't thought about it," Peta blithely replied. She'd only been working the domestic flights since she and Matt had returned from their honeymoon. Having been granted the transfer, it seemed wrong to give notice of leaving immediately.

"I've never seen a pregnant air hostess."

"I won't be showing for a while, Megan," she quickly reasoned. "And I could use the money to buy things for the baby."

"You could sell that motorbike."

Peta bridled at the critical note in her sister's voice. "It's handy for getting through the traffic to and from the airport."

"I thought you told Matt you didn't want to hang on to your career."

"So I did. And I meant it. But I haven't had the baby yet, Megan."

"Well, you don't want to take any risks when there's no need."

"Oh, for heaven's sake! I'm not a fragile flower."

"Sorry. It's just... I know how much this means to you. I want everything to go right. For Matt, as well. You will consider his feelings..."

"Megan, stop being a worrywart. Matt's fine. He's over the moon about the baby. It is what we got married for, after all."

"Peta..." A sigh. "...Don't you yet realise..." She hesitated.

The doorbell rang.

It was a good excuse not to hear any more well-meant but tiresome advice. "Got to go, Megan. Someone's at the door."

"Well...have a happy night."

"We will."

Brimming with confidence, Peta opened the door to a delivery boy whose arms were loaded with flowers.

"Mrs. Matt Davis?" he asked.

"Yes."

"For you." He grinned and passed over the flowers—a bunch of blue irises and a bunch of pink tulips. "Congratulations, Mrs. Davis."

"Thanks," she said dazedly, not having expected flowers. The memory of the rose debacle was still sharp, making her feel uncomfortable about the gift.

The accompanying card, however, instantly cheered her... Matt, being a daddy.

Consider his feelings...

Megan's advice echoed in her ears. Not that she needed it. Matt had the same feelings as herself about starting a family. A boy or a girl...she smiled in delight. The flowers were perfect. She took great care and pleasure in arranging them in a bowl to set on the table as a centrepiece for their special dinner tonight.

It turned into the happiest of times together. Somehow, because of the baby, there was an extra warmth between them, a closer intimacy. They were sharing the miracle of a new life starting, Peta reasoned.

Over dinner, they tossed names at each other,

laughing over some, seriously considering others. It was fun. It was magic.

Matt suggested they start looking for a house in earnest. His Bondi apartment was no place for a baby. They discussed what areas might be suitable, trying to keep his travel time to work within an acceptable limit. He didn't mind her keeping on her job for a while, though once they found a property they both liked, Peta wanted to spend all her time on turning it into their home.

Wonderful plans…

And when they finally went to bed, Matt was so tender, so caring, caressing and kissing her stomach, her breasts…the feelings he evoked there were exquisite…the gentle sucking… Peta cradled his head, imagining holding their child, feeling the bond of love that would form…

She forgot Megan's advice.

She didn't consider Matt's feelings at all.

She thought only of the baby she would have.

CHAPTER FOURTEEN

"MATT..."

His subconscious heard the fear in Peta's voice even as he struggled awake. The light was on, which had to mean morning hadn't come yet. He squinted at her. She was holding on to the doorway, tears streaming down her cheeks.

"What is it?" he asked, alarm jabbing through his mind.

"...I'm bleeding."

Bleeding...

At six weeks!

The next few hours were a blur of pain. Matt did his best to remain calm and comforting. The trip to the hospital and dealing with the Casualty staff was a nightmare, begging for immediate help, frantically filling out forms, waiting to hear, willing everything to be all right, fearing the worst...and Peta inconsolable when told she had miscarried.

Never had Matt felt more futile. There was nothing he could do to help. Nothing. And his own disappointment and grief cut deep. Their baby had become very real to him over the past month, with all the plans they'd made for it...their son...or daughter. Suddenly, heartbreakingly, it was not to be.

"It's nature's way of saying something was wrong," Peta's doctor said, meaning it kindly, but it only made matters worse.

Peta took it personally, as though the miscarriage was somehow her fault, though the doctor assured her it wasn't and there was no reason not to try for another baby after she'd given her body some recovery time. She was too distraught to listen to reason. She retreated inside herself, shutting Matt out, unwilling or unable to share their loss with him.

So it continued for days afterwards. She didn't go back to work though she insisted Matt should, more because she didn't want him with her than any caring for his business. Not that she said it. He felt it. There was very little communication from her...no desire to reach out and touch...no sharing. She was listless, lifeless, dead inside, barely recognising Matt's presence. Or anyone else's.

Megan tried to talk to her. No response. Her mother came to visit. It did no good. She was wrapped in sorrow and the shield was impenetrable.

For Matt it was a very black time.

His mother sympathised but had no useful advice to offer. His secretary commented that there seemed to be a high rate of miscarriages on first pregnancies these days and put it down to a lingering hormonal imbalance from many years on the pill. Matt couldn't repeat that to Peta. She was blaming herself as it was and there was no medical proof for Rita's theory. Nevertheless, it was an explanation that made sense to Matt and gave him more hope that time would resolve whatever problem had occurred.

Three weeks passed and Peta's depression did not lift. She refused to seek medical help. Attempts at offering compassion, tenderness, understanding won only blank-eyed stares. In bed, she kept so rigidly to her side, the message projected was loud and clear...*leave me alone*. She literally shuddered away from any caress, freezing him into isolation.

In sheer desperation one evening, Matt tried to goad her into an argument, anything to spark some life back into her. He'd cooked them dinner and persuaded her to sit down to it but the way she picked carelessly at the food felt like a further rejection of him.

"It's not the end of the world, Peta," he jabbed, his voice sharp with frustration.

He might not have spoken for all the awareness of him she showed. No tilt of her head. No flicker of an eyelash. Her hand idly stirred a fork around her plate and there was no discernible interruption to the movement. She had blocked him out.

Matt could feel his stress level climbing and couldn't stop it. His heartbeat accelerated. Driven to force her into paying attention, he crashed his fist down on the table.

It startled her into looking at him.

"I said...it's not the end of the world," he bit out fiercely.

She wearily turned her head away.

Blood pounded through his temples, drumming the need to attack on any ground, do whatever had to be done to re-establish contact. "I thought you were a fighter, Peta," he flung at her. "I thought if something knocked you down, you'd get up, dust yourself off, and barge straight on with living."

No response.

"This giving up...it's defeatist and destructive. Do you think I don't feel the loss, too? That it's only you...bleeding?"

For Matt, the ensuing silence stretched into unbearable tension. Their entire relationship was on the line. If she couldn't show him some shred of humanity, there was nowhere left to go.

Finally she broke it.

"If you want a divorce, just say so," she said in a dull, flat voice.

It was a killing stroke.

Even so, Matt fought against it. "You didn't tell me I only had one shot at a child with you, Peta. As I recall it, we made a bargain to try for four."

Her head jerked in anguish. "I can't go through this again."

"Life is about taking risks. If you're not prepared to face them, you might as well be dead." His voice was shaking with the turbulence inside him. He scooped in a quick breath and challenged her again. "Is that what you want? To crawl into your hole and die because you lost the first round?"

She turned to him, her eyes water-bright and wounded. "I took the risk of marrying you, of trying to make a dream happen. And this is my punishment for it."

"Punishment!" Disbelief burned into a sense of outrage. The jealousy he'd tried to suppress came pouring out in a fiery torrent. "What? Because you married *me* instead of the Latin lover who sucked you into giving him your heart to break?"

She flinched and he took savage satisfaction in striking her on the raw.

"I suppose if you'd lost *his child,* you would have sought comfort in him and there wouldn't have been any sense of punishment at all. In fact, it's me you're punishing, for not being the man you really wanted."

"Don't!" she cried in a pained little voice.

"Don't what?" he whipped back at her, hating the sense of being used and discarded. Offering him a divorce as though their marriage meant nothing! The frustrations she'd stirred poured into a bitter tirade. "Don't send you roses? Don't throw the truth in your face? Don't touch you because your body is only a vessel for a baby which I failed to deliver on?"

"Stop it!" She clapped her hands over her ears.

It was the most inflammatory thing she could have done. Adrenalin pumped through Matt. He was on his feet so fast, his chair slammed onto the floor. He picked her up, hoisted her over his shoulder and strode for the bedroom, ignoring her wild struggle to escape from him, his whole body raging with the need for some grain of satisfaction out of all he'd given to make their marriage work.

"Fight as much as you like, but you will listen to me!"

He hurled her down on the bed, pinned her body

there with his own, lifted her arms above her head and held them with a steely grip. "Cheat!" he snarled, revelling in the shock on her face.

"No..." she moaned.

"Yes! You made a lifelong commitment to me and here you are welshing on it within three months! Wanting to take off my wedding ring and walk away!"

She rolled her head in protest. "I didn't say that!"

"It wasn't me who brought up divorce, Peta."

"I only meant..."

"What?"

"I might not be able to carry a baby full term. You want a family..." Tears welled into her eyes. "It's what you married me for."

"I married you for *you*," he cried vehemently.

"Please don't make me," she sobbed, trying to squirm out from under him. "It would be rape, Matt."

Rape! If she'd smashed a fist into his face it couldn't have jolted him more. Yet the next instant he realised he was hard, his body having reacted to the volatile energy coursing through him. She was squirming away because she was frightened of his erection, recoiling from his supposed lust for her, the lust she had once said was mutual.

He picked himself off her and rolled onto the other side of the bed, deflated, defeated, drained of any will to fight on, horrified by the reaction he had unwittingly drawn from her. She moved into a scrunched-up huddle, shaking and weeping.

For a while he felt dazed, guilt, regret, shame, chasing through his mind. He was not a violent man. He'd only wanted her to talk to him. Physical force was anathema to him. For her to actually fear him, accuse him…it was the blackest hole Matt had ever fallen into.

Gradually reasoning returned, telling him he'd been driven by some survival instinct, natural enough in the circumstances. He'd fought…and he'd lost. Peta didn't want him anymore. Not for anything.

He was conscious of his heartbeat slowing to a sluggish rate. His interest in life was reduced to zero. Nevertheless, life would go on. For both of them. Though it was clear it could only be in separate ways. Touching was impossible now.

Her sobs quietened and eventually stopped. She lay still, apart from him. The apartness hurt. He wondered if it would ever stop hurting. She didn't know—never would know—how much she'd meant to him.

"I wouldn't have taken you. Not in anger," he said in justice to himself.

No reply.

He forced himself to swing his legs off the bed and stand up. "I guess you'd prefer to be alone."

No response to that, either.

There was nothing left to say.

Matt quietly collected his travel bag which was kept packed with essentials for business trips, slung a couple of clean shirts over his arm, determinedly denied himself one last look at the woman he'd married with such impetuous faith in their future together, and walked out of the bedroom. He couldn't bear to be near her anymore. She was too painful a reminder of what was beyond his reach.

In the living room he picked up his keys and wallet from the telephone table. He was at the door before it occurred to him it might not be a good idea to leave Peta alone in what he could only think of as a traumatised state, even though it seemed to have become her refuge from realities she didn't want to deal with. He shied away from the thought she might be suicidal. *He* was the problem. Remove the problem, let her feel free of it and the pressure on her would ease.

Still…concern for her drove him back to the telephone table. He rang Megan. The two sisters were close. If anyone could do anything for Peta, it would be Megan.

She answered the call.

"It's Matt." He heaved a sigh to ease the constriction in his chest. "I'd appreciate it if you'd call Peta in half an hour or so. Check that she's all right."

"Why? Aren't you there?" she asked sharply.

"I'm about to leave, Megan. She doesn't want me with her."

"Matt, please…hold on."

The plea echoed the words she'd spoken when he'd danced with her at the wedding reception… *You will hold on to her…no matter what?*

He shook his head over the blind confidence he'd carried this far. Megan must have known what shaky ground he'd embarked on with Peta…known and worried about it, hoping for the best. If the miscarriage hadn't happened…but it had…and the ground had crumbled…irreparably.

"There isn't anything to hold on to, Megan," he said, acutely aware of the hollow ache inside him.

"Can't you…" The half-spoken plea fell into a deep sigh. "I'm sorry, Matt. I guess it's gone too far," she added sadly. "I did try to pull her out of it."

"I know. Thank you. If you'd check on her…"

"Yes, I'll do that. Don't worry. And Matt, for what it's worth, I think you're the best guy she could ever have got."

His mouth twisted in irony. "Not good enough where it really counted. 'Bye, Megan. I'll be in touch."

He left the apartment and drove off into the night with no clear idea of where to go. The future was a blank to him…a huge black blank…his wife, the family they had planned, their home…all gone. Matt had never felt so lost and alone, not even when his father had died.

He thought of the baby whom nature had ordained shouldn't live…his and Peta's baby…perhaps as wrongly formed as their marriage…though it would have been loved—was loved—by both of them. A dream that wasn't to be.

But it had only been part of the dream for him. He'd loved the extra closeness it had brought with Peta…the way her eyes had shone with happiness, including him in their warm glow, the impulsive affection she'd shown when he'd suggested plans that pleased her, even her pleasure in the flowers he'd sent.

He'd come to believe she *did* feel he was special...her husband in every sense...and they were building towards what his parents had once shared...a deep and abiding love for each other...

An understanding of what his mother had felt when his father had died flooded through him. The loss...the pain...the gut-wrenching bereft feeling. He shouldn't have criticised her for losing interest in life. He hadn't had the experience to measure her grief. All those years together. He'd only had a taste of it, yet...

Tears welled into his eyes and blurred his vision. Grown men don't cry, he told himself, furiously blinking the wetness away. He pulled the car to the side of the road and parked, struggling to regain the composure to drive on. Suddenly it didn't seem to matter.

He wept.

The bleeding went on.

CHAPTER FIFTEEN

THE telephone wouldn't stop buzzing. It nagged and nagged until she was finally driven to reach out and pick up the receiver on the bedside table.

"Peta?"

She dragged in a deep breath. An effort was needed to stop the pestering. "Megan, I don't want to talk. I've taken a sleeping tablet and I'd like to sleep. Please..."

"Just one tablet?"

"Yes," she snapped, exasperated by the sisterly concern. "Goodnight."

She crashed the receiver onto its cradle and resettled herself in the bed, her back turned to the empty side, stubbornly intent on doing her utmost to block it out of her mind. She wanted—needed—oblivion for a while. Tomorrow she would think about what had happened tonight. It was too hard, too confusing, too *awful* to come to grips with it now.

Cheat!

She shut her eyes tight and willed the tormenting word to stop its relentless beat on her brain.

Cheat...cheat...cheat...

It wasn't true...it wasn't! She'd met him more than halfway in everything. Until...

He just didn't understand how much having the

baby meant to her…how devastating it was to have her body reject what she most wanted. It had nothing to do with Giorgio. Nothing!

Her arms automatically cradled her stomach. The empty place inside her ached and ached. She couldn't have borne to have sex with Matt, feeling him where she'd lost the baby. It wasn't fair of him to expect it of her…wasn't fair… The wedding ring on her finger didn't mean he could take her without her consent, even though he might think she had bargained that way…no sex without the ring.

Cheat…

No…no…

It didn't work if it wasn't mutual. At least he had realised it and let her go, left her alone, alone to the emptiness she couldn't bear and couldn't fill.

She rocked herself in anguish, rocked herself to sleep, and clung to sleep, even through a shifting blur of troubling dreams where everything she reached for moved out of reach and dwindled away into nothing.

Then there was a bell ringing, piercing and persistent, forcing her to swim groggily to the surface of consciousness. Daylight hit her eyes. She quickly closed them again. Tomorrow had come and she still didn't want to face it.

Cheat…

She writhed as the hateful word slithered out again.

The ringing sound was the doorbell. Desperate enough to grab at any distraction, Peta hauled herself out of bed, pushed her arms into her dressing gown, and tottered out to the door, wrapping the edges of the gown around her, tying the belt, running her fingers through her hair. One thing was certain. It wouldn't be Matt. He'd use his key.

She opened the door, carelessly resigned to dealing with someone. Except the someone was Megan who pushed straight past her into the apartment without so much as a by-your-leave. She was alone, no baby Patrick in tow, for which Peta was grateful, though she wondered who was minding him.

"Are you taking to sleeping through the day as well as the night?" Megan sniped, bristling with every sign of being on the warpath.

Peta sighed, wishing her sister had stayed away. "What time is it?"

"Time you came to your senses."

"Oh, don't start…"

"I'll do more than start. I'm through with your sensibilities, Peta. You've crucified a decent man and I'm going to nail you to the wall for it if it's the last thing I do!" She shot her a scathing up and down glance. "I'll grant you a cup of coffee first. And believe me, that's sisterly love!"

She'd whirled into the kitchen before Peta got her breath back from the fast and furious attack. *Crucified?* The evocative word sent a shiver down her spine. She swiftly assured herself Megan was exaggerating the situation, as she always did when she was upset. Matt must have called her, though surely he wouldn't have confided the awful nastiness of last night's scene.

Cheat…

She shuddered and hurried after her sister, finding her tipping fresh grains into the coffee-maker. "I don't know what Matt told you..."

"He called me out of concern for you, Peta." Her eyes flashed contempt. "You, who haven't given him one smidgeon of concern since you miscarried. As though it wasn't *his baby,* too."

It whipped up a hot flood of guilt and shame. She'd been so immersed in her own grief, she hadn't seen his, and he must have felt it, wanting a baby as much as she did. He'd said as much last night. She should have responded. The leaden weight in her heart had been too heavy to shift.

Megan clicked the grain-holder into place and switched the coffee-maker on with angry snaps. "I never thought I'd say this about my own sister..." She turned, her eyes stabbing home the point. "...But you're a blind, self-centred bitch, Peta."

Shock punched her heart. She opened her mouth to protest but Megan swept on.

"To take Matt's love and do what you did to him...treating him as nothing...turning your back on him...disregarding his..."

"Now hold on a moment!" Peta shot back at her, stung into defending herself. "Matt never once said he loved me."

"No, I daresay he didn't." Megan's chin lifted, defying the negative claim. "He's the kind of man who wouldn't lay that on you because you told him you didn't love him. And you've rubbed that in these past few weeks, haven't you? Rubbed it in so far you left him nothing to hold on to.''

The heat in her cheeks was scorching but Peta hung grimly on to her defence. "Love never entered into our marriage," she insisted vehemently. "From the very beginning…"

"Matt was head over heels in love with you, Peta," Megan cut in with pitying scorn in her eyes. "That was obvious to the whole family at Patrick's christening. Ask them. Ask any guest who attended your wedding. Only you were blind to it. Only you…"

"No, you're wrong," she cried, frantically resisting the charge. "He was physically attracted to me, yes. And he wanted a family…"

"With you. Because it was you," Megan pushed relentlessly.

"No." Peta shook her head vehemently. "Because he was ready."

"He loved you," Megan bored on, unshaken in her conviction. "He adored you. You were always the focus of his attention, caring about what would please you, what you wanted, doing everything he could to make you happy." She paused, shaking her head at the stupidity of not seeing. "Add it up, Peta. That's not lust. It's love in capital letters."

It was the kind of man Matt was, Peta wildly reasoned. He treated his mother the same way. The realisation struck… He *loved* his mother.

"And I'll bet my boots he thought if he gave you all your dreams, you'd come to love him," Megan went on. "But the first dream got broken and you showed him he was worth nothing to you, didn't you, Peta?''

She rubbed at her throbbing temples. She hadn't meant to hurt Matt. It was just…she couldn't…

"Never mind all he did to help you." Megan's voice kept beating at her with sickening force. "Never mind his need to share what you were both feeling and to move on from it, his need for the togetherness he thought he'd get in your marriage. He not only lost his child, you took away everything you'd promised him, as well."

Cheat…

"Matt poured out his love for you these past few weeks, Peta. It was obvious to both me and Mum he was desperate for you to *be* with him again instead of off in a world of your own. I don't know what went on between you last night, but I can guess. You must have ripped out the last shred of hope Matt had of ever reaching into your heart. And even then…even then…he cared about you…calling me so I'd check on you, to make sure you were all right."

She hadn't heard his desperation. Not really. It had floated past her. Yet the words he'd punched so angrily at her…his violent actions…

"You still want to pretend he didn't love you?" Megan mocked savagely.

"I…he never said…" Any coherent thought was lost. She lifted her hands in an agitated attempt to ward off more accusations. Her head was pounding with snatches of memories. Matt had said it…in many ways. She simply hadn't taken it in.

The last night of their honeymoon... *I don't care to have roses banned from our life... It didn't feel like a convenience to me...* and last night... *I married you for you.* She hadn't let those words *mean* what they had meant. She'd let them pass, attaching them to Matt's pride if anything, not love.

The coffee-maker pinged.

"You'd better sit down before you fall down," Megan coolly advised. "I'll bring your coffee."

Yes, she did feel faint. She drifted into the living room. The plates with the remnants of the dinner Matt had cooked were still sitting on the table, food congealed on them. She gripped the back of her chair, staring at the mess on her plate, knowing she'd made a much worse mess of the commitment she'd given to Matt.

If you want a divorce, just say so.

She'd said it so carelessly, numbly. While he...

Another shudder ran through her. She gripped the chair more tightly as she painfully acknowledged the truth Megan had shot at her. She had been blind and self-centred where Matt was concerned. His bringing up Giorgio... He'd given her every sign and she hadn't seen.

"Oh, great!" Megan snapped in disgust, seeing the state of the table. She plonked down the coffee mugs she'd brought in and whipped away the soiled dinner plates. "You can sit down now," she tossed at Peta on her way back to the kitchen.

She sat. There was no fight left in her.

Megan returned and settled at the table, all brisk

determination to set the record straight. "I've run out of sympathy for you, Peta," she started again. "You're not the only woman who's suffered a miscarriage. You were lucky it happened at six weeks."

Peta flinched. Lucky?

"Some women carry their babies much longer before losing them. Even up to six months…"

"Don't! Don't go on…with that," she pleaded brokenly.

"I can imagine the disappointment but at least it happened quickly," Megan said more gently. "And the doctor said there was no reason why you shouldn't try again."

Peta shut her mind to the argument. Everything within her recoiled from trying again. It felt wrong. Even if Matt could forgive her the hurts she'd inflicted…no, she couldn't do it.

Megan kept on talking at her.

Peta sat in pained silence, waiting for her to run down. Eventually she did, having nailed all the nails she'd come to hammer into her sister's conscience. She'd done a good job of it, Peta thought with sad and bitter irony. Too good. There was no going back from here. It wasn't a marriage of convenience anymore, not with Matt's love involved.

"You've driven Matt away from you," Megan concluded. "If you want to get him back—and you'd be a fool not to—you've got to give him a reason to…"

"No," she cut in, meeting her sister's eyes with firm decision.

Megan leaned forward in earnest. "Peta, you won't find a better man."

"It's no good," she answered bleakly. "I'd keep on hurting him. And I don't want to."

"If you just…"

"No. Go home, Megan. You've done what you came to do."

"But, Peta, if you let him go…"

"As I am right now, he's better off without me." She couldn't even satisfy him in bed. The lust they had shared wasn't in her anymore. "I won't lie to Matt. He'd know anyway." She stood up, feeling a draining sense of futility. "Please… I would like you to leave now."

Megan was frowning heavily. "You mean…all I've said doesn't make any difference to you?" she cried in frustration.

"You've made me see…what I was too blind to see. And I wish it could be different. But it isn't."

She stepped away, finishing the conversation by moving through the living room to the entrance hallway, giving Megan little choice but to follow. She did. Peta held the door open for her. Megan paused, still frowning.

"What will you do now?" she queried worriedly.

"Have a shower, get dressed, have something to eat, go for a ride on my bike."

The frown deepened. "Where?"

"I don't know. It doesn't matter." Peta managed a crooked smile. "Maybe I'll find myself along the way."

"I care about you." It was a burst of concern.

"It's all right, Megan," she assured her sister softly. "Thanks for coming. Thanks for saying all you've said. It did make me see."

Megan looked as if the stuffing had been knocked out of her. She heaved a long, ragged sigh then tried to fix some resolution. "Call me. Let me know you're all right."

"I will," Peta promised.

It was little enough but Megan took it and left, accepting there was no more to be done with all the will in the world.

Peta shut the door and leaned back against it, completely spent. Matt had shut this door on her last night. She'd driven him away and no matter how empty her life felt, she could not go to him, not to use him as she had, ill-using him in the end.

She knew how it felt to be cheated in love.

She wouldn't do it to him.

CHAPTER SIXTEEN

MATT finished his breakfast and cleaned up, impatient to be gone, out of his apartment and on his way to work. He felt a constant, miserable sense of emptiness here, with Peta gone. The apartment was still as functional a place as it had ever been, handy for everything, but stripped of her belongings, her feminine bits and pieces, her perfume, her presence…it was a painful reminder of what he didn't have.

Still, it had only been a month since she'd left, scrupulously taking nothing of his with her. *If* he didn't count the short span of his life they'd spent together. That was gone, though he couldn't get it out of his mind. This apartment held the imprint of both the best and the worst of it.

He really should look for another place to live. Yet he couldn't bring himself to let it go. Couldn't bring himself to let *her* go, he corrected himself. Which was damned stupid, considering the ring of finality in the note she'd left behind.

I'm no good to you, Matt. I'm sorry. Truly sorry…

What use was *sorry?* It showed a measure of caring, he supposed, though she'd shown precious little caring towards him. People said *sorry* when they didn't know what else to say, a nicety thrown out to cover not actually doing anything.

He shook his head and moved briskly into action, collecting what he needed for work. Five minutes later he was in his car and facing the usual morning traffic snarl. It was worse this time of year with Christmas coming up and shoppers eager to start the day early. Matt schooled himself to be patient. Nothing was going to move until it was ready to move.

The trip from Bondi to Taylor Square went at snail pace. However, once he was on South Dowling Street, the run towards the airport and Rockdale moved more smoothly. Stopped by a red light, he watched a Qantas jet coming in to land at Mascot and wondered if Peta was on it. She'd gone back to work. Megan had told him so the one time he'd called to ask about her.

Which meant the depression had lifted. Matt was glad of it for Peta's sake, but getting herself together had obviously made no difference to how she viewed their marriage. Or him. He supposed the next contact she made would be about a divorce.

The light turned green and the traffic moved. His car phone rang. It was his mother calling.

"I was wondering what to do about Christmas, Matt."

"Whatever you want to do, Mum," he answered, totally disinterested in the festive season.

"Well... I hate asking you this, but you haven't said...is there any chance of you and Peta getting back together?"

Matt grimaced. He hadn't talked about it to his mother because he was too acutely conscious of the doubts she'd voiced about their marriage and he couldn't bear her saying, "I told you so."

"It isn't likely," he said shortly.

"Then..." She hesitated, aware she was on sensitive ground. "...It's not likely we'll be spending Christmas with the Kelly family? It's just that they did invite me...at the wedding."

"Better let it go, Mum. Make your own plans," he advised, silently mocking himself for handing out advice he couldn't take himself.

"All right, dear. I'm sorry..."

"Not to worry," he quickly assured her. He'd had a gutful of *sorry*. "I'll call you later in the week and you can tell me what you want for Christmas." She always did.

"That would be nice, Matt."

He breathed a sigh of relief as she ended the call. He didn't want to talk about Peta. It screwed him up. Much better to bury himself in work. They certainly had enough of it at the factory with the Christmas rush. Extra orders for logo T-shirts were pouring in. He had a full day ahead of him, thank God! He needed to work to the point of exhaustion where he didn't notice the emptiness in the bed in his empty apartment.

"Flight attendants, please take your seats for landing."

Peta was glad to sit down and buckle up. The early morning three-hour trip from Cairns to Sydney was a busy one for the stewardesses—serving three hundred breakfasts to people reading cumbersome newspapers, then cleaning up afterwards. She would be glad to get home and have a couple of days off, too. The run of flights to far North Queensland were unsettling.

Having to stay overnight in Cairns, so close to Port Douglas where she and Matt had spent their honeymoon, inevitably triggered memories. They'd had a wonderful time together. Not even the black pit she'd fallen into after the miscarriage could cast a shadow over the fun they had shared before she lost the baby. When she thought of the various men there'd been in her life, Matt had definitely been the best companion, in every way.

She missed that companionship now. Very badly. Even the intimate aspect of it. Lust or love…the pleasure of it had been quite intense at times. A month ago, she couldn't have believed she would crave it again, but she did in the lonely stretches of the night, especially last night, remembering the wild satisfying of each other's every desire on their honeymoon.

A rueful sigh escaped her. They were probably flying over Rockdale right now, coming in to land. Matt would be on his way to work, or there already, snowed under with business. Christmas was a prime opportunity for merchandising.

She shied off the thought of Christmas, a family day, for children. Matt was probably going to hate it this year, too.

She'd done him terrible damage.

Impossible to undo it.

The plane touched down and gradually decelerated along the tarmac. Peta switched her mind back onto her duties. Once the passengers were disembarked, there was the business of checking in, but it wouldn't be long before she was off for the rest of the day. Maybe she would call Megan and see if her sister was free for a visit.

She was in the staff room, on the point of leaving the airport, when one of the pilots casually commented, "Oh, there was a guy asking after you, Peta."

"A guy? Who was he?"

The pilot shrugged, then grinned teasingly. "Tall, dark and handsome."

Matt? Her heart leapt and catapulted around her chest. "Is he still here?"

"Don't know. I told him what door you'd be coming out of."

"Thanks."

Her mind buzzed with a mixture of alarm and excitement. Why would Matt come for her here? What did it mean? Maybe he intended to pick her up and carry her off. Matt was certainly capable of doing that...a wild impulse, a cavalier sweeping away of all objections. If he did...could she let him? She wanted to...right or wrong she no longer cared. She desperately wanted to have Matt with her again.

But was he still here?

Agitated, exhilarated, and almost scared to look, she hurried out of the staff room and into the terminal. She swung her gaze around in hopeful anticipation, and her fluttering heart stopped dead.

It wasn't Matt waiting for her.

It was Giorgio... Giorgio Tonnelli...as elegant as ever in what was undoubtedly an Armani suit, wearing the self-possessed air of a man whose strikingly handsome face naturally drew admiring looks.

As weird as it seemed, after the initial shock of seeing him here, in Australia, Peta felt completely disconnected from him.

Even though his dark eyes hotly consumed her, she didn't melt. Her heart didn't race. She couldn't even summon up the sense of having once belonged to him for two whole years of her life. The only emotion he raised was a stomach-turning disappointment that he wasn't Matt.

He lifted his arms in a gesture of *here I am for you.* It evoked an instant inward recoil. No urge to run to his embrace. Not the slightest temptation, either. It seemed almost grotesque that he should invite it, expect it.

It was gone—all gone—the effect he'd had on her.

When she remained standing stock-still, he stepped closer, smiling his intimate smile, murmuring, "*Carissima...* I have missed you so much."

The velvet voice made her bristle. A voice full of deception. Not like Matt's, always sounding direct and open and honest, meaning what he said, following through on it, a voice she could trust.

"What are you doing here, Giorgio?" she demanded, resenting the reminder of how he had fooled her, and what a fool she had been to let *him*—a mannequin of a man—come between her and Matt.

His eyebrows slanted appealingly. "I have come all

the way from Milano to see you again. You were the light of my life, *bella mia.* These past few months..."

"No business deal pending?" she cut in, seeing him as Matt would—the Latin lover, pouring out romantic words that had no real substance to them.

He shrugged. "I did a little manipulation to make this opportunity."

More lies. He obviously wanted a convenient little fling with her while he was here. *Convenience...* That's what she'd been to Giorgio, not to Matt. How had she let this man flatter her into believing him? All he had was superficial glamour.

"Well, I'm glad your trip won't be entirely wasted," she said dryly. "As I told you before, we're finished. If you'll excuse me..."

"No..." Ruffled by her cool rejection, he grabbed her hands, meaning to press them into submission. His fingers brushed over her rings. They startled him into looking down. "What is this?"

"I'm married!" Peta stated proudly, lifting her hand to flaunt the beautiful diamond Matt had given her.

She should have taken it off, given it back. The wedding ring, too. It wasn't right to keep them. Yet, removing the last link to their marriage had seemed...heartless, another hurt on top of too many hurts. It would have to be done, of course, when it felt right.

"This cannot be." Giorgio's dark eyes blazed with fierce, emotional intensity. "It is me you love. You cannot have forgotten. *I* have not forgotten."

"I never loved you, Giorgio," Peta said with very clear certainty, totally unmoved by the flow of energy he was trying to wrap around her. "I only thought I did because I didn't know any better."

The truth finally came to her, bursting into her heart and exploding through her mind. "My husband has taught me what love is. And I'll love him for the rest of my life," she vowed, breaking away from the man who had no right to hold her.

Her heart was racing now.

The insight—revelation—about her true feelings for Matt was so strong it couldn't be doubted. She loved the man she had married. Loved all that he was.

If she hadn't been so hung up on Giorgio when she and Matt had first come together, if she hadn't been so hung up on having a baby…blind, blind, blind! She'd had the right man, her mate in everything, and she'd blown the chance of a lifetime.

She broke into a run, out of the terminal, across the road to the taxi rank. She didn't know how to fix the damage she'd done. Matt might throw her out of his office. She couldn't blame him if he did. But she had to go to him and beg for another chance, convince him somehow that she did love him.

Otherwise…

No, she wouldn't think about otherwise. There'd been too much negative thinking already. She had to be positive. Very, very positive.

So she had to stop shaking with the fear that she'd left it too late, stop thinking of herself. It was Matt she had to concentrate on…his concerns, his needs, his desires, his dreams. That was what love was about. He'd shown her. And maybe, if she was very, very lucky, he might show it to her again. After she'd shown him.

CHAPTER SEVENTEEN

MATT was immersed in paperwork. He heard the office door open. Rita bringing him coffee, he thought, and welcome it was, too. This computer printout was giving him a headache, it required so much concentration.

The door closed. Odd action for Rita. No smell of coffee, either. He looked up, frowning at the break to his mental summary of the figures in front of him.

Peta stood against the door.

The shock of seeing her where she wasn't supposed to be made him question his vision and sanity for a moment. But she *was* real. Neither memory nor imagination could conjure up the sheer vibrancy that emanated from her. It choked him. Peta…as stunningly beautiful as she'd always been to him, and looking so vital, glowing with an energy that seemed to sparkle all around her.

A cramp hit his heart.

The sparkle couldn't be for him. Something else must have brought her here. She was wearing her Qantas uniform, either going to or coming from work. A drop-in visit. She held a tissue-wrapped bundle in her arms—a sheath of flowers? It made no sense to him.

He stared at her eyes, so vividly blue, sharply alert,

searching his almost fearfully, unsure of her welcome, yet there was bold determination in her stance, blocking the door, virtually challenging him to say something about it.

The tumult of feeling she stirred made silence the easier course. Let her speak first since only she knew why she'd taken this initiative. But she didn't speak. Her throat was moving convulsively. He noticed the fast rise and fall of her breasts. Shallow breathing.

She *was* afraid of his reaction to her. Matt hated that. Peta had no reason to fear him. None at all. He would never have raped her. The very idea sent a wave of revulsion through him, driving him to put her at ease.

"You're looking well, Peta," he said, managing an ironic little smile.

"I hope you don't mind my...my intrusion," she gabbled out.

Just don't say you're sorry, Matt thought fiercely, feeling he would lose what composure he had if she did.

He effected a shrug. "Your choice. I regret that I overrode your choice to ignore me on our last night together. Please feel free to do or say whatever you like, Peta. I don't really go in for molesting people."

Hot colour raced up her neck and burned into her cheeks. "I know I was a blind, self-centred bitch," she shot at him, a writhing shame in her eyes. She took a deep breath and softly added, "Especially after the miscarriage."

Matt sat absolutely still, hit by the sheer unexpectedness of her harsh self-accusation. He didn't know what to make of it, didn't know how to respond.

"I hope… I hope you can forgive me, Matt."

The plea triggered a wild rush of hope. Had she come because she wanted their marriage to continue? Caution clicked in, suppressing the impulse to offer her anything she wanted. Her conscience was troubling her. That was all. She needed to be at peace with it. To read anything more into a plea for forgiveness was asking for another rejection.

"It was a distressing time. For both of us," he said quietly. "What's gone is gone, Peta. Don't worry over it on my behalf."

The words rang in Peta's ears like a death knell. *What's gone is gone…* It was what she'd found with Giorgio. If Matt felt the same way, she didn't have a chance.

But it hadn't been real love with Giorgio, she wildly reasoned. Real love didn't die. Even though she'd done her unwitting best to kill it, surely it could be revived. Matt and she were still the same people.

She loved him. How could she not have known it before? He sat there behind his desk, in charge of his world, emanating the strength to carry any responsibility, the power to make his vision happen. The character of the man was stamped on his face, mirrored in his eyes…steady, reliable, tough when it came to survival but with a readiness to be kind, to care for others.

She loved him. And he was so beautifully

male...his shirt stretched tight over his broad shoulders, sleeves rolled up revealing his muscular forearms, hands lying in repose on the desk, their long fingers capable of the most extraordinary sensitivity. Her gaze fastened on his mouth...

She ached for him to kiss her as only he could, firing the passion they'd known and shared, the intimate possession of each other, the wild hot glory of it and the delicious sensuality he always drew her into. That couldn't be gone. She wouldn't let it be gone.

Matt struggled to contain himself. Why didn't Peta say something? His nerves were stretched to the limit, waiting for her to make some further move, either towards him or away. Her eyes had roved over him as though...no, he couldn't let himself believe that.

Yet his whole body was on pins and needles, reacting automatically, instinctively, and the way she was now staring at his mouth...the desire to leap up and do a powerful piece of molesting was pumping through his heart so fast, his feet started to tense into springing action.

She moved, walking forward, speaking at the same time. ''I've been such a fool, Matt, not realising what I had in you, wasting what you gave me. I guess I needed this past month apart from you to get everything in perspective.''

Her voice warmly pleaded, her eyes craved his understanding. The positive signals almost exploded Matt's mind. She wanted him back.

"I brought you these...to show you I've come to my senses."

She laid the tissue-wrapped bundle on his desk. It held roses. *Red* roses. Matt shook his head in bewilderment. Was it a peace offering, an attempt to erase bad memories, or did they mean what she'd said they should mean? He looked up to scan her eyes again, urgently questioning.

She gave him a tremulous smile. "I love you, Matt. I hope you can find it in your heart..."

He exploded onto his feet, his chair flying back on its rollers. "Peta..." Her name encompassed all the yearning he'd tried to stifle. He couldn't find the voice for anything else. A few strides around the desk and she was in his arms—heaven in his arms.

Her mouth met his with her lips parted, wanting what he wanted, and she flung her arms around his neck and arched her body into his as though she was as starved for him as he was for her. He kissed her, kissed her with all the pent-up passion of the hours and days and weeks when there was no outlet for his yearning, no relief, no joy in anything because she wasn't there for him.

But she was now. And the miracle of it overwhelmed him. He cupped her face, holding it back so he could drink in the reality of her again, see that what she said was still true. Her eyes swam with his own rampant feelings. He couldn't find words to tell her how much it meant, how much she meant to him. All he could do was hug her tightly, imprinting her body on his again, feeling her warmth and softness and the beat of her heart against his, revelling in the scent of her, the sweet giving of herself.

She sighed. "Matt, I am deeply sorry for..."

"Don't!" The words came tumbling out of the wretched soul-searching he'd done. "I knew you were fragile under your strength, Peta. That you were still shattered by what had happened to you. I took the risk of marrying you, telling myself I was strong enough to carry us both through anything. And I was wrong. I lost patience. I lost..."

"No. I was lost, Matt." She tipped her head back to meet his eyes, and reached up to tenderly stroke his cheek. "I should have held on to you until I found myself again," she said softly.

"Perhaps it was better for you to have a breathing space," he excused, so relieved the rift was over he was happy to excuse anything.

Her eyes were eloquently grateful for his understanding. "I was so afraid I'd hurt you too much and you wouldn't let me into your heart again."

"You've never been out of it, Peta. Not from the moment we met," he answered simply.

"The moment?" She looked amazed.

He smiled in sure self-knowledge. "My life instantly started to revolve around you. When you stopped Father O'Malley from continuing the wedding ceremony, I almost died of a heart attack, then and there."

She shook her head in bemusement. "I was determined to marry you, no matter what. My mind got it right, Matt." She grimaced. "Unfortunately, my heart didn't catch up with it until I realised how empty my life was without you."

"It's okay." He grinned, brimming with happiness. "All I care about is having you with me again."

"It will be better this time around," she promised fervently.

He cocked a teasing eyebrow. "I don't know that some things can be bettered."

She laughed and wiggled provocatively. "I told Rita we weren't to be disturbed."

"How thoughtful of you!" She was deliberately inciting arousal. Not that Matt needed encouragement. But it was great she had no inhibitions about showing him he was wanted as well as loved. "And did Rita agree to this arrangement?"

"No question about it." Her eyes flirted wantonly with his. "She said you were working yourself to death and needed to be saved."

"And did she say she'd hold the fort until the rescue mission was completed?" Matt slid a hand around to free the buttons on her blouse. "It may take some time. You have a desperately hungry man here."

Her hand started burrowing between them at waist level. "I'm ready for emergency action." Her eyes danced wickedly. "In fact, I came prepared for it."

"You did?" he quizzed, enjoying the banter, loving her boldness, revelling in the excitement it generated.

She grinned. "I'm not wearing pants."

Matt's heart did a sky leap into his throat. It was their wedding day all over again, yet there was a brilliant freedom from doubt and fear in this gift of her-

self that lifted it into a joyful new start for both of
them, a better start, injected with a deeper knowledge
of each other, the experience of having come through
a crucible of pain, and what they were—what they
had together—was still there, bonded so much more
strongly this time.

"How do I love thee?" he murmured, the sheer
pleasure of her overwhelming him. "Let me count the
ways."

He did it with his hands, his mouth, his body and
soul, with every touch, every caress, every kiss, and
he felt her response coursing through every part of
him, like a stream of sweet soothing, like a river of
no return, like a torrent of tumbling passion, like a
sea of rolling ecstasy.

The thought of conceiving a child didn't once enter
Peta's mind. She was filled with the man she loved,
the man who loved her, and it was a fullness that
needed nothing else, a fullness that wanted nothing
else.

At the core of it was a deep, deep gratitude that
they had found each other, that Matt was still here for
her, wanting her, loving her, tapping a huge welling
of love for him. It gushed through her in great waves,
a flood of feeling that swelled her heart and flooded
her mind and washed her soul free of any sense of
loss.

This was the real start of their marriage.

The promises didn't have to be spoken.

She felt them.
And knew them to be real and abiding.

They were joined once more and time and place meant nothing to Matt. The soaring togetherness transcended everything else. Only when the sense of fulfilment allowed room for other senses did his vision take in the roses cushioning Peta's head, and their heady scent filled his nostrils, spreading the joy of ultimate harmony.

Roses...
Red roses...
For love.

CHAPTER EIGHTEEN

FOUR children were unthinkable, Matt decided.

One would have to be enough.

"You're it, Timothy Andrew," he muttered to the day-old infant who was snuffling around his chest, clearly working up to making a demand for something his father couldn't supply.

Peta was fast asleep and Matt was determined she should stay asleep. She needed all the recovery time she could get after the long, traumatic labour of giving birth. He himself was still in a state of shock, appalled by the pain she had suffered in producing this incredibly tiny bundle of humanity. He'd been emotionally battered and physically drained just watching her go through it. Torture. Absolute torture.

"You just hold off, Tim," he commanded, shifting his baby son up to his shoulder and patting his back for comfort. "Curb your instincts for a while and consider your mother. You pushed her to the limit getting born."

Though it wasn't Tim's fault, Matt conceded. Both he and Peta had been madly keen on having a child. Tim had had no say in it at all. And it was great to have a son, no doubt about it. Nevertheless, the result did not justify the means, in Matt's newly informed opinion.

In fact, he'd like to go back to the prenatal classes he and Peta had attended and shove the real truth down those instructors' throats, make them all have babies themselves so they knew their breathing control lessons were impossible to apply when it came to the crunch.

If only he had the power he'd revolutionise the hospital system, too. This idea of having the baby staying in the room with its mother all the time might be fine for bonding, but when was the mother supposed to get some sleep? If there weren't nurses coming in to check off their charts, the baby needed attention. If he weren't here to protect Peta from constant interference in the holy cause of entrenched hospital routine, she'd probably be dead from exhaustion.

It was ridiculous. It was inhumane. There should be a rule that a nurse couldn't be a nurse on a maternity ward unless she'd had a baby. He'd already drilled two brisk, unsympathetic nurses on that point and shot them out of here, demanding someone with a bit of understanding tend to his wife. He didn't care if he was labelled a "difficult husband." He'd vowed to look after Peta and he would.

Tim started sucking on his shirt. Matt figured frustration would set in any moment now and for a tiny baby, Tim had a great pair of lungs. Bound to be a good swimmer when he grew up. In the meantime, he only knew to use them for yelling. Matt short-circuited the imminent impulse by heaving himself out of his chair and walking up and down the room, softly singing "Waterloo," an old ABBA song he remembered from his childhood.

"Winning the war, Matt?"

Peta's amused question startled him out of his absorption in serenading his son. She was wide awake and smiling at him. Matt shook his head in amazement. It was beyond him how she could smile at anything after yesterday's dreadful ordeal but she seemed to manage it quite naturally.

"Merely staving off attack," he answered ruefully. "Tiny Tim was trying to gobble up my shirt."

"Give him to me. It's past his feed time."

"I didn't want to wake you."

"I feel more rested now, thanks Matt. You've been so wonderful through all this."

Him wonderful? He was a nervous wreck, barely hanging on. He didn't understand how Peta could look so serene as she took their baby and set about feeding him. Tiny Tim had no problems though. He latched onto one of the best parts of the world and obviously knew it was heaven-sent. A chip off the old block, Matt thought, as he relaxed back in his chair and watched one of the miracles of nature.

He was so tired he almost nodded off. A tap on the door brought him alert again. The instant rise of aggression faded as the visitor proved to be Peta's mother, not an officious nurse.

"Mum! How lovely!" Peta cried in surprised pleasure. "I wasn't expecting you until tonight."

Nanna Kelly—her choice of grandmotherly name—handed Matt gifts for the baby and hurried to Peta's bedside, gabbling excitedly. "I couldn't wait for your father. I caught the train down. My goodness! Doesn't he have a lot of hair?"

Peta laughed.

She actually *laughed*.

"Black. Like Matt's. Isn't he beautiful?" she crowed proudly.

As the two women discussed his son's beauty, Matt sat in stunned silence. Except for that one black period after the miscarriage when Peta had, as she'd said, lost herself, she was a fighter, capable of standing up to anything and boldly moving forward. He knew that, yet he was staggered by the way she seemed to have put yesterday's pain behind her.

"I hope you're not too disappointed, Mum," he heard her say.

"Disappointed?" Matt echoed incredulously. "Why should she be?"

"Remember John's fourth was another boy," Peta answered equably. "Tim is the eighth grandson in a row, Matt. Mum was hoping for a girl."

"It truly doesn't matter, dear," her mother assured her. "As long as he's healthy."

Matt approved this sensible sentiment. If Peta's mother wanted another granddaughter she could look to Megan or John or Paul to provide it.

"He's absolutely perfect, Mum," Peta crooned. "Maybe we'll be lucky enough to have a girl next time."

Matt couldn't believe his ears. Next time? How

could Peta contemplate a *next time?* Had she somehow contracted amnesia?

His mother arrived next. Harold, her friend from
the Bridge Club, had driven her down from Gosford.
Harold was beginning to feature very strongly in his
mother's life. She had come a long way from the
health farm.

She took one look at the baby and cried, "Oh! He's
the spitting image of Matt!"

Peta laughed. *Again.* Maybe it was some form of
euphoria that came after the safe delivery of a baby,
Matt reasoned.

"There's certainly no doubting who his father is,"
Peta agreed, smiling at him with a glow of love that
made his heart turn over.

His mother bestowed a benevolent smile on him,
too. It spurred Matt into a response. "Sorry it's not a
girl, Mum," he said, remembering she had fancied
buying pretty things. Both Nanna Kelly and Grandma
Davis had apparently been thinking pink. "You'll
have to make do with a boy." Especially since
Timothy Andrew was the only grandchild she was
going to get.

"Well, dear, I'm sure you and Peta will have as
much joy in your darling little son as your father and
I had in you," she replied warmly.

"We certainly will," he agreed. "I was just thinking of your pleasure."

"You mustn't mind me, dear." To his astonish-
ment, she actually blushed. "I'm afraid I won't be
available to do much baby-sitting."

Matt couldn't quite swallow his surprise. "Are you telling me, after years of nagging…"

"Now, Matt, you did say you weren't having a baby for my sake. I'm very happy for you and Peta. Delighted that everything's turned out so beautifully. And he's perfect. Absolutely an adorable baby…"

A "but" was hanging in there somewhere.

"Isn't a grandson good enough for you?" Matt demanded irritably.

"Of course he is!" she protested, shocked he could think otherwise. "I know I'm going to love our Timothy to bits. And when I *am* home…"

"You're going away?"

"I was trying to tell you…" She looked as coy as a young girl. "…Harold has asked me to go travelling with him. And I thought…why not?"

Matt found himself bemused by this unexpected turn in their friendship. "You're right, Mum. Why not?" he reasoned. He'd preached not hanging on to the past and she'd been a widow for over three years now. If Harold's companionship rounded out her life, she should take it.

His mother heaved a sigh of relief. "I'm so glad you don't mind, dear."

"It's your choice, Mum," Matt declared, hoping it would work out really well for her.

Her cheeks pinked up some more. "Since there seemed no point in wasting time—we're not getting any younger—we've already decided on a tour and it's only a month before we're off."

Matt had to smile at the repetition of his own argument about wasting her life. "Where are you off to...Europe?"

"No... no... I did that with your father."

Apparently Harold was not to tread on that ground.

"We're taking a boat down the Amazon," she announced, her eyes lighting up at the thought of it.

"You're what?" Surprises were coming thick and fast.

"It will be such an adventure, Matt."

His mother...the adventuress! A little over a year ago, she could hardly be persuaded out of her own home!

"After that we're planning a cruise to Alaska."

"Alaska," he repeated numbly.

"Then there's a wonderful wildlife sanctuary in Kenya."

"Okay!" Matt held up his hand. "I've got the picture. You now have lots of things to live for. You don't need a grandchild."

"Of course I need a grandchild," she cried, not realising he was teasing her. "I'll just love telling Tim about these marvellous places when he's old enough to understand."

"We'll all be interested to hear about your adventures, Cynthia," Peta put in warmly.

"Dear Peta..." His mother looked benignly upon his wife. "...You make a beautiful mother."

"Thank you." Another smile. "I don't know if I could bear to leave Tim with a baby-sitter so don't let Matt make you feel guilty."

"It is hard to let go," his mother said sympathetically and settled herself on the bed for a cosy chat. "Now you must give me your advice on my hair, Peta. I won't be able to go to a hairdresser for weeks on end once I'm off." She reached out and tenderly stroked Tim's hand. "Oh, to have skin like a baby's! Isn't it glorious?"

Matt rolled his eyes and retired to the sidelines. Women, he decided, were definitely from another planet. Peta was glowing as though she hadn't been anywhere near death's door barely twenty-four hours ago. Her mother was probably mourning the fact that pink was not the order of the day, never mind the miracle that her daughter had survived. As for his own mother...well, he had wanted her revitalised, but how could she be rattling on about herself when she, of all people, knew what it took to bring a baby into the world?

She had to remember almost dying in childbirth. Matt certainly hadn't forgotten what he'd so recently experienced. He now understood what his father had felt, watching his wife dice with death.

Megan arrived.

There were now four clucky women, drooling over his son and saying not a word about how he'd come into the world. Was it some kind of sisterhood conspiracy? They'd all had the experience of birth, in one form or another, so they instinctively agreed to forget it? Once survival and motherhood was achieved, that was it?

Then he heard the most incredible words he'd ever

heard in his life. From Megan! Who was the one most recently to have given birth before Peta.

"Only twelve hours of labour and no stitches. You really got it easy, Peta," she said blithely.

It was too much for Matt.

"Easy?" He climbed to his feet as his voice climbed upwards. "Easy? Are you mad, Megan?"

Four female faces turned to him in startled wonderment, as though none of them had any idea why he should be upset.

"I was with Peta every minute of those twelve hours," he thundered. "And let me tell you none of it was easy."

"It's over, Matt," Peta said gently.

"I was only comparing it to the twenty hours I went through," Megan explained reasonably. "And having to cope with six stitches where I tore."

"Tore..." Matt gulped the word and closed his eyes, struggling to come to terms with a blasé description of torture. "How..." He scooped in a deep breath and glared at all of them in disbelief. "...How can you dismiss it as though it were nothing? It was absolute hell watching Peta in agony."

His mother sighed. "Just like his father." She gave Peta a wise look. "My husband used to faint at the sight of blood. You'll have to watch that with Matt if you're going to have four children, dear."

"We are not going to have four!" Matt shouted. "If you think I will let Peta go through that another three times..."

"Matt, the first is always the hardest," Peta said indulgently. "It usually gets easier with each one."

"Yes. My fourth came so fast we barely made it to the hospital," her mother chimed in, then looked wisely at her daughter. "Men never cope with pain as well as women do."

"You're right, Mum," Megan said, frowning thoughtfully. "I'd forgotten about Rob being all shaken up at Patrick's birth. Maybe they shouldn't let fathers in, though I must say it was good having Rob's hand to hang on to."

"And sharing in it," Peta said, giving Matt an appealing smile. "It did help, having you with me all the way."

Confusion set in. Total confusion. "You mean... you actually want to do this again?" he challenged her, reaching for some grain of sense.

She smiled down at their baby son. "To have another three like him, I'd do anything."

Love...

It was written on the soft curve of her lips, the glow on her cheeks, the luminous wonder in her eyes.

Matt melted.

Who was he to deprive three unborn children of a love like that?

Especially *his* children.

"Well, if you say it's all right, Peta, I guess it's all right," he said gruffly.

Though he made a mental note to take proper pain management lessons and learn what relief could be given that was absolutely safe. There had to be more than rhythmic breathing.

Peta grinned at him. "There's no point in having our lovely big home if we don't fill it with family."

She was using logic on him now.

Matt knew when he was beaten.

Four, he thought.

God help him!

CHAPTER NINETEEN

Two years on…

The medical orderly loaded Peta into a wheelchair in between labour pains. They were only three minutes apart. Matt restrained himself from giving the guy a hurry up. Peta had told him he must behave this time and let the hospital staff do their job.

"Darling, you don't have to come with me," Peta rushed out between deep breaths. "You got me here safely. I'll be fine now."

"I'm not leaving you," Matt said grimly as they set off for the labour ward.

"You could go back to Timothy."

"Mum and Harold are looking after him."

"I only meant…well, I'll be fine. You don't have to stay."

"I'm staying."

Wild horses couldn't tear him away. He had to make sure everyone did everything right. He had to hold on to Peta's hand. She was not going to face childbirth without him at her side. He had to look after her.

He checked his watch. Three hours so far. The pains had come a lot faster this time. He prayed there weren't going to be another nine hours of it. Two years had not erased his memory of Timothy's birth.

Inwardly he quailed at facing it all again but outwardly he was determined to remain like the Rock of Gibraltar. She'd said it helped if he shared it and share it he would.

They reached the labour ward.

For every minute of three long hours, Matt gave the performance of his life, soothing Peta, encouraging her, having his hand squeezed to pulp. He only cracked a couple of times, saying a few terse words to doctors and nurses in the heat of the moment. But he covered up fairly well, assuring Peta everything was going fine even when he felt like screaming abuse at everyone for not being able to hurry things up.

Then his daughter was born.

Mari Claire.

The doctor handed the tiny baby to him to give to Peta.

"It's a girl," he said proudly as he laid another child with a great pair of lungs in the eager crook of Peta's arm.

"Mari Claire," she crooned, then smiled up at Matt. "Thank you. I do so love you, Matt."

"Love you, too," he murmured, melting with so many wonderful emotions, he almost did forget the pain.

He checked his watch.

Six hours.

The labour time had been halved! The next one might only be three hours altogether!

He grinned down at his beautiful wife. "I can do it."

"What?"

"Get to a family of four."

She laughed. Matt loved her laughter.

Love and laughter, he thought.

More than anything they made life worth living.

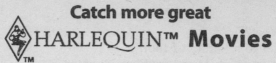 

HARLEQUIN® Temptation®

He's strong. He's sexy.
He's up for grabs!

Harlequin Temptation and
Texas Men magazine present:

1998 Mail Order Men

#691 THE LONE WOLF
by Sandy Steen—July 1998

#695 SINGLE IN THE SADDLE
by Vicki Lewis Thompson—August 1998

#699 SINGLE SHERIFF SEEKS...
by Jo Leigh—September 1998

#703 STILL HITCHED, COWBOY
by Leandra Logan—October 1998

#707 TALL, DARK AND RECKLESS
by Lyn Ellis—November 1998

#711 MR. DECEMBER
by Heather MacAllister—December 1998

Mail Order Men—
Satisfaction Guaranteed!

Available wherever Harlequin books are sold.

HARLEQUIN®
Makes any time special ™

Look us up on-line at: http://www.romance.net   HTEMOM

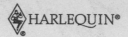

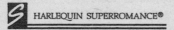

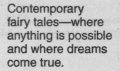

**SEXY, POWERFUL MEN NEED
EXTRAORDINARY WOMEN WHEN THEY'RE**

Destined for Love

Take a walk on the wild side this October
when three bestselling authors weave wondrous stories
about heroines who use their extraspecial abilities to
achieve the magic and wonder of love!

HATFIELD AND McCOY
by HEATHER GRAHAM POZZESSERE

LIGHTNING STRIKES
by KATHLEEN KORBEL

MYSTERY LOVER
by ANNETTE BROADRICK

Available October 1998
wherever Harlequin and Silhouette books are sold.

HARLEQUIN®
Makes any time special™

Silhouette®